MOTIVE FOR MURDER

MOTIVE FOR MURDER

Anthea Fraser

Chivers Press
Bath, England

•

Thorndike Press
Waterville, Maine USA

This Large Print edition is published by Chivers Press, England, and by Thorndike Press, USA.

Published in 2002 in the U.K. by arrangement with the author.

Published in 2002 in the U.S. by arrangement with Juliet Burton Literary Agency.

U.K. Hardcover ISBN 0–7540–4698–2 (Chivers Large Print)
U.K. Softcover ISBN 0–7540–4699–0 (Camden Large Print)
U.S. Softcover ISBN 0–7862–3689–2 (General Series Edition)

All characters in this publication are fictitious and any resemblance to real persons, living or dead, is purely coincidental.

The text of this Large Print edition is unabridged.
Other aspects of the book may vary from the original edition.

Set in 16 pt. New Times Roman.

Printed in Great Britain on acid-free paper.

British Library Cataloguing in Publication Data available

Library of Congress Cataloging-in-Publication Data

Fraser, Anthea.
Motive for murder / Anthea Fraser.
p. cm.
ISBN 0–7862–3689–2 (lg. print : sc : alk. paper)
1. Authors—Fiction. 2. Private secretaries—Fiction. 3. Large type books. I. Title.
PR6056.R286 M68 2002
823'.914—dc21 2001053033

PROLOGUE

This morning, my daughter came into the room holding a copy of Matthew's book, *Motive for Murder*, and at once all the memories, faded over the years, came rushing back.

'Wasn't it through this book that you met Dad?' she asked, as, taking it eagerly from her, I began to flick through the pages.

'That's right. Goodness, how formal it all was then—Mr this and Miss that.'

'And presumably not a word processor in sight?'

'Goodness no, this was bashed out on the old steam typewriter.'

Sophie perched on the arm of the sofa, looking at me curiously. 'Didn't you tell me once that there was some trouble while it was being written?'

I nodded, suddenly sober. 'Three people died during the course of that book. In fact, the writing of it was as much a story as the book itself.'

'Then why not write about that?' Sophie suggested. 'You know, "The Making of *Motive for Murder*." Everyone does it nowadays, and people would be interested—it's become a classic, after all.'

I looked across at her, startled. 'Oh, I

couldn't!'

'Why not? You say there's a story in it.'

'But it was so much a part of all our lives.'

'An autobiography, then. Oh, go on, Mum! You said you'd be at a loose end when I go to university—here's a way to fill in your time. And don't try to update it—write it as it was then: formality, typewriter and all.'

I made another token protest, but the idea was taking root and, with it, a feeling of excitement. By going through it all from the beginning, perhaps I'd be able to glimpse the first, misty hints of what was to come; hints that were too obscure to notice at the time.

I went on flicking through the pages, the memories growing stronger. This was the chapter I typed after the swimming incident; this one while Kate was there. Long-forgotten incidents flickered at the back of my mind; I probably remembered more than I'd realized.

By supper time, I'd decided to give it a try. And I'll dedicate whatever results to the shades of those no longer with us—and, of course, to my husband, who very definitely is.

CHAPTER ONE

The sun was just breaking through the early morning haze and it promised to be another long, hot day. Under the lofty ceilings of Paddington Station, however, the chill of dawn still lingered and I shivered in my thin dress, wrapping my coat more tightly about me.

'Cold?' Gilbert asked, turning from the booking office and handing me my ticket. His eyes were concerned.

I shook my head, and lifted my chin.

'Emily—don't go!' He hadn't put it into words before. He took my arm and led me briskly into the buffet. 'We've time for a coffee,' he insisted, as I hung back to glance anxiously up at the clock.

'You don't really want to go, do you?' he said, when we were sitting looking at each other over the steaming cups. 'It's just a question of pride now.'

'Nonsense.' I drew a long, steadying breath. 'It's the chance of a lifetime!'

'We don't know anything about this chap,' he went on frowningly, staring into his cup. 'I can't think why Father agreed to it—but you can always twist him round your finger.'

'On the contrary,' I said, 'we know a lot about him.' The coffee had warmed me and both my voice and my resolution were stronger. 'Item one:' I ticked off on my fingers, 'Matthew Haig is one of the country's leading novelists. Item two: he needs a secretary for three months to help him with his latest book. Item three: he lives in Cornwall—which, incidentally, is a wonderful place to be in this kind of weather.'

'Item four:' Gilbert interrupted, 'he's been your ideal ever since you read his first book at school, and you won't admit that when you actually met him, you didn't like him. But it's true, isn't it?'

I was silent. It had always been the same; I'd been able to fool Mother and Father on occasion, but never Gil.

He reached over, his warm, strong hand on my wrist. '*Please*, Emily.'

I was surprised at the urgency in his voice. 'Don't fret, brother dear,' I said lightly, 'there's a housekeeper, a nanny and a little girl, so I should be safe. I'm not going to be buried away alone with him—and even if I were, I should probably still be safe—the dislike appeared to be mutual.'

'Then why did he engage you?'

'Perhaps the others were no better,' I suggested. 'And he's desperate for a secretary. Really, Gil, stop worrying. I'm a big girl now.'

But he didn't smile as I'd expected. He said slowly, 'I can't put it into words, but I have a feeling of—oh, I don't know. I'd just be much happier if you decided against going to

Cornwall.'

I stared at him in amazement. Dear, down-to-earth Gilbert, with a feeling he 'couldn't put into words'. It was not like him to be fanciful.

The loudspeaker boomed, making us jump.

'Heavens, come on! I'll miss it!' I stood up and for a moment longer he sat staring at me.

'Then you won't change your mind?'

'Not a chance! Now come on, there's a love, and see me off with good grace!'

The train was in when we arrived at the platform, and the late holiday crowds were streaming into it.

'Lucky we reserved you a seat,' Gilbert said.

He climbed ahead of me into the carriage and swung my case up on the rack. Then he handed me my magazine, kissed my cheek, and jumped back down on to the platform. 'Emily, if there's anything that worries you—anything at all—phone home and I'll come straight down. Do you promise?'

'What could possibly worry me? I'll be fine, really.'

A whistle blew farther down the platform and there was the sound of slamming doors. The train shuddered, rocked, and started to inch forward.

'Take care,' Gilbert said, and I nodded reassuringly.

'Goodbye!'

I waved out of the window till we rounded a bend and he was out of sight. Behind me, the compartment had filled, and my own place was the only empty one. I sat down and smoothed the pages of my magazine with fingers that shook a little. Strange, that Gilbert should be so much against my going to Cornwall, and Matthew Haig.

About me, my fellow travellers settled down for the long journey. I sat back, watching the dusty suburbs slide past with increasing speed, and my mind went back over the last few weeks to the advertisement that had appeared in the evening paper.

> 'Writer in Cornwall requires residential secretary for three months. Mutually acceptable salary.'

It had been an airless, sweltering day in London and the dusty offices of Messrs Penshurst and Dacombe had never seemed so dull. I'd spent the best part of the day helping Marcia with a conveyance and I was thoroughly bored and dispirited.

'Cornwall!' I'd said to her on the train home. 'That's the place to work!'

'Well, write after it then.'

I stared at her. 'Shall I?'

'Why not?'

Why not, indeed? Together we composed a crisp, efficient application, giving my typing and shorthand speeds. I sent it off the same evening and then, convinced I would hear no more, forgot it. A week later the typewritten note arrived. Matthew Haig would be grateful if Miss Emily Barton could attend for an interview at the Grafton Hotel on Tuesday next, 29th August.

Matthew Haig! I could hardly believe it. As Gilbert remarked, I'd been an avid reader of his books long before he became so widely acclaimed. Now, he was established as one of the foremost writers in the country, and it was he who wanted a secretary!

I made tentative enquiries at the office. My own boss was away in South America for three months and I was tired of whittling away the time by helping out the other girls. Would a leave of absence be feasible? I should be back in time for Mr Dacombe's return after Christmas. The office manager hummed and haaed, consulted the partners, and finally vouchsafed the opinion that they could see no reason why I should not take a temporary job, provided I gave them a month's notice if I decided against returning to them.

Seething with excitement, I presented myself at the Grafton, cool and, I hoped, efficient-looking in my grey linen dress. And there my elation dissolved.

Cool I may have been; Matthew Haig obviously was not. The heavy green curtains had been drawn across the window to keep out the sun, but the resulting airlessness struck me in the face like a blast from an oven.

The man at the table had removed his jacket and rolled up his shirt sleeves, but there were beads of perspiration on his forehead and his face was blotchy with the heat. A pile of cigarette stubs, some only half-smoked, filled the ashtray at his elbow, and an empty water-jug and glass stood beside it.

He did not look up as I entered, but waved vaguely in the direction of the chair in front of him. My self-confidence ebbed away, wilting in the oppressive heat. I sat down and waited. A fly buzzed aimlessly over the table, the whirr of its wings the only movement in the room. Matthew Haig turned over the page in front of him. He had still not raised his head. I began to wonder whether the message that he was ready for me had been a little previous. Cautiously I settled back in my chair and looked across the table.

I had seen his picture on the dust cover of his books, but the face in front of me was sterner, more rebellious than the facile photograph had shown. There were grooves from nose to mouth and tiny lines fanned out from the corners of his eyes. Now, as he frowned down at the papers before him, the mouth was hard and unyielding. A strong face, I decided; attractive, but disillusioned.

'Well, Miss Barton.'

My eyes lifted guiltily to his, as though he had been able to read my thoughts.

He was regarding me appraisingly. 'Your

shorthand and typing speeds seem adequate.' He paused, apparently for my comment, but I could think of none. I'd been under the impression that my skills were more than 'adequate'.

He leant back in his chair, studying me in his turn. 'The position is this: I'm working on a book, and I need someone right away. Would you be able to start at once?'

Quite suddenly, I was not sure that I wanted to. The old-fashioned courtesy of Messrs Penshurst and Dacombe seemed all at once infinitely preferable to working for this man, who was abrupt to the point of rudeness.

'Well?'

'I—think so,' I stammered, furious with myself.

'Then perhaps you'd make up your mind. I'm anxious to get on with my work as soon as possible, but I can't concentrate if my secretary is unsettled. If it would be too quiet for you at Touchstone, or you feel on reflection that you would not be suitable for the job, please say so now. There have already been—interruptions—in the course of this book.'

Put like that it was a challenge, as though he'd carelessly tossed the job at my feet and was not particularly interested in whether or not I accepted it.

I said a little stiffly, 'I don't mind the quiet, and I'm sure the work would be very interesting. I've read—'

‘You realize, of course, that it’s a residential position?’ he interrupted. ‘It’s no good thinking of taking lodgings in Chapelcombe, because I work irregular hours, often in the evenings, and Touchstone is some way out of the town. Of course—’ a flicker of sardonic amusement—‘you will be suitably chaperoned. My daughter and her nurse live with me, as well as the housekeeper.’

‘I’m aware of that,’ I said, furiously conscious of my heightened colour. My father had made enquiries before allowing me to attend the interview.

He stared at me a moment longer, then he reached out and closed the file in front of him. ‘All right,’ he said.

I hesitated. ‘You’ll—let me know?’

‘The job is yours, if you think you can do it.’

‘I’m sure I can,’ I replied with dignity.

* * *

I moved restlessly. The sun which had been so constant a companion in London for the last month had given way, as we moved west, to a dull oppressiveness. The air thickened, and by the time we reached Cornwall about two o’clock, we were in the midst of a thick sea mist which blotted out everything. So much for the sunny south.

The last of the other people in the compartment had left the train at Plymouth; a browning apple core and a crumpled newspaper were all that remained of them. I was alone, hurtling through the mist to an isolated house and a man I did not like.

Some of Gilbert's unease washed over me. Why had I let myself be stung into accepting a job which, in the moment of truth, I'd found I did not want? Pride, as Gil had rightly deduced. I could not, whatever the cost, have looked across the table at those dark, assessing eyes, and whispered humbly that I had changed my mind.

Time passed. I sat huddled in my corner seat staring out at the mist and thinking forlornly of home—comforting and uncomplicated. The rhythm of the train changed, slowed, then ground to a jerky halt.

'Chapelcombe!' shouted a voice out of the mist. In a panic I pulled down the heavy case, wrenched open the carriage door, and half-fell out. The white, drifting shroud enveloped me, clogging the breath in my throat. A whistle blew. Behind me the train lurched, responding to the signal like a rusty old war-horse. It lumbered away along the length of the platform and disappeared. My last link with London and Gil had gone.

No one else seemed to have left the train at this stop. I heaved up my case and started uncertainly in what I hoped was the direction of the exit. Perhaps the ticket collector or someone would find me a taxi. I put the case down for a moment to change hands, and the sound of hurrying footsteps reached me.

'Miss Barton?'

I jumped. My own name had somehow been the last thing I expected to hear in this eerie place. But perhaps Mr Haig—I strained my eyes in the direction of the voice, and was in time to see two figures materialize; one tall and broad, the other small and slight.

Under the smudge of the lamp they came into focus: a man with his coat collar turned up, the mist lying thickly on his hair, and a little girl of eight or nine who clung to his hand, staring up at me.

'You *are* Emily Barton? I'm Mike Stacey, and this is Sarah. I've got the car outside.'

He held out his hand and its warmth enveloped my cold fingers.

'Oh, that's wonderful,' I said gratefully. 'I was just wondering how to find a taxi.'

He picked up my case and I followed him and the child through the barrier and out of the little station to the yard beyond. A large old saloon stood waiting, roomy and comfortable. The little girl climbed into the back and her companion swung the heavy case easily into the boot. Then he came round and opened the door for me.

'You'll have to excuse Matthew, it would never occur to him to arrange for you to be met.' He climbed in beside me and slammed his door. 'Luckily, Sarah told me you were expected today. Well, now that we can see each other, hello again!'

He turned towards me and smiled. The mist was shut out of the car, and in the white light we looked at each other. I hoped he liked what he saw as much as I did. He was a few years older than I, probably twenty-seven or eight, with thick brown hair that had the hint of a wave in it. His eyes were grey and laughing, and fringed by the longest eyelashes I'd ever seen on a man, but their dreaminess was contradicted by the firm mouth and strong, jutting jaw.

'Are you a friend of Mr Haig's?' I asked, as he turned back to the controls of the car.

'His cousin, actually. I live at Chapel Farm, farther along the headland.' A quick grin. 'Matthew doesn't really approve of me!'

I raised my eyebrows but he did not elaborate. We were climbing now up what was presumably the High Street. Shop windows starred the mist and bent figures hurried along the pavements.

The child spoke suddenly. 'Miss Barton's going to sleep in Linda's room.'

Beside me Mike moved involuntarily and his foot came down hard on the accelerator. The old car lurched forward with a surprised grunt.

'Who's Linda?' I enquired.

'She was Daddy's secretary, too. She—'

'Sarah poppet, did I tell you Pinkie's had

her litter? If you come over tomorrow you can see them.'

'Oh, yes, that'd be lovely!'

'Pinkie's our prize sow,' Mike said to me. 'Sarah's known her since she was a piglet herself—Pinkie, that is!' He laughed, and I smiled dutifully, but I was wondering why he'd not wanted the child to speak of my predecessor.

The car climbed laboriously up the long hill out of town, cleaving its way through the mist like the prow of an old ship. On a fine day, there would probably be a magnificent view from up here.

'Do you get much of this mist?' I asked. 'It's been lovely in London all month.'

'Not really—it's a bit humid just now, though. The beginning of autumn, I suppose.'

We turned left up an opening I had not even been able to see.

'Almost there now.'

Left again, between some gateposts, and the car stopped. I sat still, clutching my handbag, reluctant now to leave the companionship of the car and meet Matthew Haig again.

'Well, in we go!' Mike said cheerfully.

I climbed out and shivered as the cold breath of mist enfolded me again. Mike opened the boot to get my case and I stood waiting for him, staring up at what I could see of the house. The grey stone wall rose imposingly in front of us and disappeared into the mist a few feet above our heads. The front door was set back in a recess flanked by two bay windows, and above it late roses clung to the stone like sodden blotting-paper.

Mike and Sarah came up to me, and the three of us started for the door. As Mike reached out a hand, it was opened from inside and an elderly woman stood there, tutting with distress at the weather and our damp condition.

'There you are, Mr Michael, sir. I thought I heard the car. And you must be Miss Barton, dearie. Sarah, my lovely, Miss Tamworth's been looking for you all over!'

She shepherded us inside like an anxious hen, ineffectually trying to brush the drops of moisture off my sleeve and feeling Sarah's long hair. 'Now, take these wet things off, all of you, and I'll show Miss Barton to her room. Give me the case, sir.'

'No, no, Mrs J., I'll take it. Emily, this is Mrs Johnson, Matthew's housekeeper and a treasure beyond price!'

'Get along with you, sir!' said Mrs Johnson delightedly.

'Sarah? Is that you?' A sharp voice sounded from above us, and a woman appeared on the staircase that rose gracefully at the far side of the hall.

Sarah pulled a little face at Mike and answered meekly enough, 'Yes, Tammy.'

'You'd no right to go off like that without

telling me! I've been looking everywhere for you, and your tea's been ready for over half an hour.'

'It was my fault, Tammy,' Mike said quickly, as the woman reached the foot of the stairs and came towards us. 'I asked her to come with me; I was afraid Miss Barton wouldn't entrust herself to me if I were by myself!'

The woman's face softened slightly. 'For which we couldn't blame her,' she said briskly, and held out a hand to me. 'How do you do, Miss Barton; I'm Olive Tamworth. I hope you'll be happy here.'

'Thank you,' I stammered. Miss Tamworth, though roughly of the same age as Mrs Johnson, was entirely different. The housekeeper was comfortably stout and motherly, with grey hair which escaped in little curling tendrils from her bun. She had a gentle wrinkled face, Cornish blue eyes, and a general impression of softness.

Miss Tamworth, on the other hand, was small and neat, sharp-featured and angular. There was no softness about her; not a curve in her body that I could see. But for all that, I imagined that the briskness covered a warm heart, particularly where Sarah was concerned.

'Straight upstairs now and brush your hair before tea,' she was saying. 'And you'd better give it a rub with a towel first. Why hadn't you the sense to wear your hood?'

'Where's Mr Haig?' Mike enquired, picking

up my case and starting for the stairs.

'In the library, I believe.' Miss Tamworth's tone implied that he could not be expected to rush out to greet a new employee.

Mike winked at me, and we went up the stairs in convoy. As we did so, I saw that the hall was not square, as I'd thought, but an inverted L-shape. Just short of the stairs, a small passage branched off to the right, ending in a handsome stone fireplace with an oriel window on each side of it, and two big leather armchairs. A pottery vase full of leaves stood in the empty hearth.

'The library's down there,' Mike said, seeing the direction of my glance. 'I'll take you to Matthew when you're ready.'

Mrs Johnson opened the door directly opposite the stairhead and stood to one side for Mike and me to go in. He put the case on a stool. 'I'll wait for you in the hall,' he said, and left me with the housekeeper.

'Well now, miss, I think you'll find all you need, but if I've overlooked anything, you only have to ask.'

'Thank you,' I said. It was pretty room, gay with chintz curtains and an armchair beside a gas fire.

'There's a wash basin behind the screen,' Mrs Johnson pointed out, 'and the bathroom is down the corridor to your right. We usually have the main meal at mid-day, but Mr Haig ordered dinner for tonight, in case you hadn't had a proper meal on the train.'

'That was kind of him,' I murmured.

'It will be ready at six-thirty, miss.'

Mrs Johnson withdrew. I glanced at my watch. It was a quarter to six. I went over to the window but the mist still blanketed the view. My head was beginning to ache.

I washed my face, made up again quickly, and was starting to brush my hair when there was a knock on the door and Sarah peeped round.

'Are you ready to come down?'

'Almost. Come in.'

She needed no second invitation. 'I sleep next door,' she volunteered. 'That way—' with a nod of her head. 'Tammy's opposite me, but Mrs Johnson's the luckiest—she sleeps downstairs, in a room off the kitchen.'

'What fun!'

'Yes. But she's only here during the week; at the weekends she goes to her daughter in Chapelcombe.'

'And who does the cooking then?'

'Tammy, and she doesn't like it. She says it's not her place.' The child's light voice unconsciously took on the older woman's clipped tone and I felt my mouth twitch.

'She didn't mind when Mummy was here,' Sarah added casually, 'because there were always parties and things. She used to be Mummy's nurse, you know.'

'Oh!' I was slightly taken aback by this

confidence. I'd gathered from the cover of his books that Matthew Haig's marriage had been 'dissolved', and wondered if the child missed her mother.

'Ready?' she asked again.

'Yes.' I stood up with a quick glance in the mirror, and followed her down the stairs.

Mike was waiting for us in one of the leather armchairs. Sarah went for her belated tea, and Mike, taking my elbow, led me to the library door. 'Cross your fingers!' he whispered, and knocked.

'Yes?'

Mike pushed the door open and we went in together. Matthew Haig was sitting at his desk, and he looked up with a frown. His eyes rested fractionally on Mike's hand, still on my arm, then went to my face. I was confused to feel it grow hot.

He stood up. 'So you're here, Miss Barton.'

'I met her at the station,' Mike said.

Matthew's eyes flickered to him, with an expression I couldn't read. 'Thank you.'

'It was a pleasure.' Mike smiled at me. 'Well, I must be getting back. ' 'Bye, Emily, see you soon.'

I felt, rather than saw, Matthew's raised eyebrow at the use of my first name.

'Goodbye—thank you.' The door closed behind him, and for the second time that day I felt deserted.

Matthew Haig and I stood looking at each

other. He was wearing an olive green sports shirt, long-sleeved and soft-collared, with no tie. It made him look younger than he had in London, but no more agreeable.

'Sit down.'

I did so, and he resumed his seat behind the desk. 'Have you been shown your room?'

'Yes, thank you. It's—very pretty.'

'We'll begin work tomorrow, but you might like to take these notes with you and glance through them this evening, to give you an idea of the plot. There's a rough draft of the complete novel, and the first two chapters in fair copy. This was as far as—Miss Harvey had got.'

'She left in the middle of the book?' I hadn't realized that.

He shot me a look from under his brows. 'Yes.' His voice ruled out further comment. 'Regarding daily routine, I work in here from nine to twelve each morning. The afternoons are free—I usually play golf. Then I like to start work again at five. We generally eat at midday, and have something on a tray in the evenings. However, I've asked Mrs Johnson to serve a meal in the dining-room tonight.'

'Yes, she told me. Thank you.'

He glanced at his watch. 'It should be almost ready. I imagine Mrs Johnson's just waiting for Sarah to get to bed.'

There couldn't be many eight-year-old children in bed by six-thirty. No doubt Sarah was glad an evening meal was the exception rather than the rule.

'Are there any questions you'd like to ask?'

'I don't think so, thank you.'

'Then we might as well go in search of dinner.'

He pushed his chair back and led the way along the passage to the main hall.

Mrs Johnson was coming out of the kitchen. bearing a succulently smelling steak and kidney pie. 'It's just ready, sir,' she said in her soft, Cornish burr.

At Mr Haig's gesture, I followed her into the dining-room. It was a large, impressive room, oak-panelled, with an ornately-carved mantelpiece and hunting prints on the wall. Down one side, a series of long windows looked over the garden—not, today, an inspiring view—and on an end wall, the large bay I had seen from the front of the house curved gracefully out into the mist. I shivered before I could stop myself, but if Mr Haig noticed, he gave no sign.

Miss Tamworth came in behind us and the three of us took our places at one end of the long dining table.

The meal, excellent though it was, was not a comfortable one, being eaten almost entirely in silence. Opposite me, Miss Tamworth's eyes never left her plate, and at the head of the table, Matthew Haig gazed down the length of the room into space. I was devoutly thankful, like Sarah, that this need not be endured every evening. I thought wistfully of the family meal at home, with all of us eager to tell of the day's happenings. This evening my place would be empty. I remembered Gilbert's misgivings, and a small knot of depression formed inside me.

The sweet course was duly served. The hot food had made me sleepy and my jaw ached with the strain of not yawning. The headache which had begun earlier throbbed in my temples with persistent pain.

At last the meal was over. I said tentatively, 'If you don't want me this evening, Mr Haig, I think I'll go to my room. I'm rather tired after the journey, and I'd like to unpack before going to bed.'

'Yes, of course. I'll get you those notes to take up with you.'

I went with him to the library and he handed me a sheaf of papers. 'Good night, Miss Barton. I hope you . . .' he paused, and seemed to change what he'd been about to say: '. . . sleep well,' he finished lamely.

'Thank you.'

I went up the long staircase to my room and thankfully closed the door behind me. Someone, presumably Mrs Johnson, had drawn the curtains and lit the gas fire, and the little room was warm and welcoming. I slipped off my shoes and dropped the notes on the bed. I'd have a bath, unpack, then settle down to read the typescript.

Lying blissfully in the hot water, I thought idly about the people in the house and wondered what my predecessor had made of them. I wished I could meet Linda Harvey, and remembered Mike's reaction when Sarah had mentioned her. Matthew Haig hadn't been very forthcoming either, but surely it was unusual for a secretary to leave in the middle of a book? Perhaps he'd had to dismiss her.

The bath had refreshed me and I no longer felt so tired. Back in my room I unpacked quickly, folding clothes away into drawers and hanging dresses in the cupboard, impatient now to read through Mr Haig's manuscript. Finally, having slid the empty suitcase under the bed, I was free to settle down in the chintz chair with the typewritten pages.

CHAPTER TWO

I awoke the next morning to find the room filled with golden light, and slid out of bed to run to the window. My room was at the front of the house, and immediately below lay the gravel drive leading to the gateway through which I'd driven with Mike. On either side of the drive, lawns as smooth as billiard tables stretched away to distant laurel hedges.

I'd hoped to catch a glimpse of the sea from my window, but in this I was disappointed.

Beyond the boundaries of the garden lay moorland, rising to the left, and on the right dropping down to the road up from Chapelcombe. A heavy dew lay on the grass but all trace of the mist had gone.

I turned from the window, picked up the zipped writing-case which I'd laid on the table the previous night, and climbed back into bed with it. This seemed the ideal chance to write my duty letter home.

> *Well, I arrived safely,* I began conventionally, *and was met at the station by Mr Haig's daughter—who's about eight—and his cousin (very good-looking!). Touchstone is quite a big house, but I haven't seen it properly from the outside because, believe it or not, it was shrouded in mist when I arrived! However, it's quite imposing, and set in stately, formal gardens surrounded by clipped laurels.*
>
> *My bedroom is small and pretty, and I've just woken up. Last night, I read through the hundred or so pages of the draft novel and it's fascinating—a murder story, which is unusual for Matthew Haig, but with the sympathetic characters that are in all his books. Which is strange, because in real life he doesn't seem to like people much!*

I paused. Outside the window a bird was singing, but there was no other sound.

It's to be called MOTIVE FOR MURDER, I went on, *and from what's been written so far, I think the idea is to tell the story of a murder from five different angles; that of each suspect in turn. They all have motives, and it will be a challenge for the reader to guess which one actually committed the crime.*

A knock on the door interrupted me, and Mrs Johnson came in with a tray of tea. 'Oh, you *are* awake, miss. 'Tis a lovely morning, and all that nasty mist gone, praise be.'

'It looks wonderful,' I agreed, laying aside my letter and taking the tray from her. 'Thank you. I was hoping I could see the sea from my window, but I can't.'

'Not quite, no, but it's not far away. Just down the slope and across the Chapelcombe Road. Now miss, there's breakfast in the dining-room at eight for Miss Tamworth and the liddle lass. Mr Haig has toast and fruit juice in his room. Would you like something up here, or will you go down?'

I eyed her over the teacup. 'What did Miss Harvey do?'

Mrs Johnson started, and her quick, apprehensive glance dropped from my steady gaze. 'Miss Harvey? Well now—well, I seem to remember she changed her mind each day. Sometimes she went down, but latterly—' She broke off, confused, and rubbed her palms on her apron.

'Latterly?' I prompted gently.

Mrs Johnson kept her eyes down. 'Latterly she didn't want no breakfast at all, miss.'

'Oh.' I regarded her meditatively but apparently she was not to be inveigled into speaking of Linda Harvey, either. I thought of the dim, silent dining-room of the evening before—it made a poor comparison with my bright bedroom.

'I'd like breakfast here, please Mrs Johnson, if that's all right. Toast and fruit juice would be lovely.'

'Very good miss,' Mrs Johnson made her thankful way to the door. 'And Mr Haig said to remind you he'll expect you in the library at nine.'

'Thank you.'

The door closed behind her and I frowned to myself, mentally adding another paragraph to my letter.

There appears to be some mystery about the girl who was here before me—nobody wants to talk about her.

But I couldn't write that, of course: it would worry them. I was not, however, going to let it worry me.

I had another drink of tea. This was better than dashing off to the tube, I thought with a smile. Breakfast in my room, and a leisurely stroll to the library when I've finished! And the plot of the novel was far more fascinating than the dry legalities of the office I'd left behind. This afternoon, when I was free, I would go and look at the sea. Linda Harvey, whoever she was, must have been mad to let a job like this slip through her fingers.

* * *

At five minutes to nine I knocked on the library door and went in. Matthew Haig was already at his desk. He barely glanced up. 'Good morning.'

'Good morning, Mr Haig.' I laid the typescript on the desk in front of him.

'You got through it all right? Good. Well, there's a lot of stuff on the tape that I've done in the last few weeks since—I haven't had a secretary. We won't waste time on that now, because I want to start dictating, but perhaps you'd type it out as soon as possible.' He motioned me to sit down. 'I usually dictate until about midday, then for the last hour before lunch you can type out your notes. That should give you plenty of time—I don't get through much new work in a day.

'In the afternoon, as I think I told you, I play golf, and as long as you're up to date with your notes, your time is your own. You'll also have two free evenings a week. Is that satisfactory?'

It was, of course, very satisfactory; despite the evening work, these were shorter hours than I'd been used to. His brusque manner, though, made it sound as if he was interviewing a somewhat inadequate charlady. 'Quite, thank you,' I said.

'Right, then we'll start. Incidentally, I shall expect you to keep me straight—tell me if I change the colour of someone's eyes in midstream, or repeat myself.' His mouth lifted slightly in what might be taken for a smile, so I dutifully smiled back.

We began to work, and despite his claim not to go quickly, I was kept busy, cursing myself for not having looked up the outlines of such words as 'murder', 'deceased' and 'mortuary', which were new to my shorthand vocabulary.

Some coffee arrived at eleven, but Matthew did not pause in his dictation, and a thick layer of skin had formed before I was able to ease my cramped fingers and drink it.

At last, just on twelve o'clock, he leant back in his chair. 'Right, that'll do for now. Work from the tape first, then this morning's work. Leave them on my desk when you've finished.'

He stood up, and without further comment left the room.

On the opposite side of the hearth stood another desk, which was presumably mine. A covered typewriter stood on it, and on a table to one side was the tape recorder. I put paper in the machine, switched on the recorder, and began to type.

I was only about half-way through the first tape when Mrs Johnson looked round the door to say it was ten minutes till lunch. It seemed, I thought ruefully, as if my afternoon walk to the cliffs would have to be postponed.

I glanced out of the window in time to see Sarah come running over the grass, with Mike strolling behind her.

She was aiming for the front door, but on seeing me she swerved and motioned me to open the French window. 'Oh Miss Barton, Pinkie's got the loveliest little babies!' she cried excitedly. 'Uncle Mike let me hold one and it was all warm and velvety!'

I'd forgotten Mike's promise to show her the piglets—in fact, it had registered in my mind only as an attempt to stop her chatter about Linda Harvey.

'How's it going?' he enquired now, coming up to us. 'Is the muse co-operative today?' He was smiling and the admiration in his eyes lifted my heart.

He really was remarkably handsome, with his thick hair and those grey, incredibly long-lashed eyes. I was struck again by the paradox of their dreaminess and his lean cheeks and strong, square chin. 'The muse has about three weeks' start on me, I gather,' I replied. 'It will take me some time to catch up.'

'So you won't be free this afternoon?'

It was merely a question, I told myself, not a veiled invitation. 'Afraid not, and I was hoping for a closer look at the sea.'

'There'll be plenty of time,' he said easily.

Behind me, loud through the open window, the dinner gong sounded.

'Away you go, both of you, or there'll be trouble. I'm off to the Chapel Arms for a pint. See you! 'Bye, Sarah.'

'Thank you for showing me the pigs!' Sarah called over her shoulder, and he raised a hand in acknowledgment.

'Uncle Mike likes you,' Sarah remarked as we hurriedly shared the cloakroom basin to wash our hands.

'Does he?' I hoped I sounded non-committal.

'Yes, he was asking me about you.'

Miss Tamworth appeared at the open door. 'Hurry, Sarah. Oh, I beg your pardon, Miss Barton.' Her eyebrows conveyed surprised displeasure at the shared washbasin. Sarah flashed me a conspiratorial grin and followed her across the hall to the dining-room.

Well, I had two friends here, I thought to myself, and perhaps that wasn't so bad for less than twenty-four hours.

* * *

Lunch was not much more cheerful than dinner had been. However, Sarah's chatter helped lighten the atmosphere, despite repeated commands not to talk so much and to eat her food while it was hot.

Matthew spoke only once, to enquire whether I had finished the notes. I told him I had not, but would do so after lunch, and he made no comment.

Accordingly I spent the long, golden afternoon typing, first to the tape recorder, and then from my shorthand notes. The pile of pages grew gratifyingly and by four-thirty I had finished. There was half an hour in hand before the evening session, and I badly needed some fresh air.

I went out through the French windows and across the smooth lawn to the gates through which, in the mist, Mike had driven me last night. Today, it was a different world.

On my left, the rough road petered out into a sheep track, meandering farther up the hill among tufts of grass and golden fronds of bracken. Autumn was already touching the spiky hedgerows, and jewel-red berries studded the green, but this afternoon it was still summer and the air was heavy with the warm, honey-sweet smell of gorse. Along the path a grasshopper whirred and a clumsy bee droned lazily among the clover at my feet. For a moment I debated whether to take the moorland path, but the call of the sea was strong in me.

I turned down the hill and after a few

minutes came to the wider road which led up from the town. Beyond it lay the cliffs and the sea.

I crossed quickly, almost running now my goal was in sight. But almost immediately I realized I had not, after all, time to reach the beach and be back at the house by five. The sand lay a long way beneath me, reached apparently by means of a flight of steps cut out of the cliff which fell away almost at my feet.

To my right an outcrop of rock ran out into the sea, cutting off the little bay below me, and beyond it lay the main beach of Chapelcombe. It would probably be possible to walk round the rocks at low tide, but now the water was right up, and with it the glorious salty tang which I missed so much in London.

I sat down on the warm grass, clasping my knees and gazing out across the water while I breathed deep, ecstatic lungsful of air.

The water was calm and blue, dotted with tiny sailing ships like a child's painting. Below me at the base of the cliffs the rocks rose pinky-grey, wearing a ruffle of drifting foam. Two seagulls glided lazily, their wings still. And all this was mine, for three whole months!

Down in the town the church clock chimed a quarter to five. Reluctantly I pushed myself to my feet and stood for one last moment drinking in the peace of it all. Then I turned and walked back to the house.

The library seemed dim now, with the

golden light all at the front of the house, and I shivered as I sat down at my desk, wondering if I had time to run upstairs for a jumper before Matthew arrived. I hadn't; at that moment he came into the room.

'You're ready—good. Are you up to date?'

'Yes, Mr Haig. The papers are all on your desk.'

'Did it take you the whole afternoon?'

'Almost; I just had time for a quick walk to the cliffs. It's a lovely little bay down there, isn't it? I'm looking forward to a swim one afternoon.'

He lifted his head quickly. '*Can* you swim?'

The question was abrupt, and I looked at him in surprise. 'Yes. Why?'

'Oh, no reason.' He looked a little disconcerted. 'Just—take care, that's all. The tide can be treacherous, even in the bay.'

'It looked like a mill pond today,' I said.

'People have been known to drown in mill ponds.'

I stared at him. Could he be serious? 'Only with stones round their necks!' I said with a nervous laugh.

He did not reply, and my silly little joke hung embarrassingly on the air between us.

'Get your notebook,' he said, and I was glad to do so. Damn him, I thought, as my pencil sped over the page. Why does he have to make me feel so uncomfortable, so unsure of myself? Perhaps Linda Harvey knew what she was doing, after all.

CHAPTER THREE

The next few days fell into the same pattern. Mornings and evenings were spent in the library with Matthew. I was relieved to discover that his frugal-sounding 'something on a tray', which he'd told me comprised our supper, was in fact a pretty substantial meal, consisting of ham, eggs and fried potatoes or a plateful of smoked haddock. Lunch was by then a dim memory, and I was never back in time for afternoon tea—if, indeed, any was provided. Those suppers in the library, stilted as they were, made a welcome break in the concentrated work which engrossed me as much as it did Matthew.

The afternoons, once I got into the routine, were my own, and though I enjoyed myself exploring my new surroundings, if there was a half-formed hope of meeting Mike in my mind, I was disappointed.

When the wind blew in from the sea I abandoned the stinging sand and climbed instead up the sheep-track to the moors. They were filled with an exultant solitude that at once soothed me and made me restless. After the crowds of London, it was almost unearthly to be able to spend a whole afternoon walking, alone with sun and wind, and to meet nobody. Up there, the petty irritations of my hours with Matthew and the niggling unease I felt about Linda Harvey dissolved into the air.

Over behind the town, I could see the outer reaches of the golf course where Matthew played, and from one hillock it was possible to look right down on the chimneys of Touchstone. It seemed as if I could jump directly on to the roof. The smooth lawns, the laurel hedges, the neat vegetable garden, and even the minute figure of Mrs Johnson hanging out the washing, lay at my feet like a discarded toy.

I stood for several minutes staring down at it all with the wind in my face. Suppose it really was a dolls' house, full of puppets. Jerk the string and the puppets danced; drop it, and they fell lifeless to the ground.

I shivered suddenly, turned away and ran down the hillock, startling a clump of silly sheep which had inadvertently approached. They bucked clumsily out of my way, their white faces staring, and moved off together, pushing and bumping aimlessly into each other. I stood looking after them until they were no more than large blobs of cotton-wool among the scrub. Down here beneath the hillock it was sheltered from the wind and the sun still held the heat of summer.

I stretched out on the short, prickly grass and lay back with my hands behind my head, staring up at the scudding cloud-sheep against the deep blue of the sky. Bees murmured, a cricket hummed. My eyelids drooped. Somewhere high in the air the song of a lark cascaded down like liquid music. How lucky I was, I thought drowsily, to have this job—and how unlucky was Linda Harvey, to lose it.

A cloud skidded over the sun, and without its warmth I was suddenly cool. I sat up. It was as though the day itself frowned and retreated at the name of Linda Harvey. I laughed aloud at the idea, but among the still grasses the sound was a discord. Beating wings clapped behind me and I spun nervously round as some bird I had startled rose from the heather. The peace of the afternoon was spoilt. I stood up, dusted down my dress, and was about to start for home when I heard the sound of a car.

It was so totally unexpected up here that for a moment I wondered if it was, after all, a plane. I was not long in doubt. It was definitely a car, and near at hand. I ran in the direction of the sound and up another rise of ground. To my surprise, I saw that about five hundred yards away a road dissected the moorland. It was low-lying, between high banks—probably following some ancient river course. As I watched, the car swung into sight and passed beneath me. I shaded my eyes to watch it, wondering where the road led to. Probably some farm or other. Of course—it would be Mike's! He'd said he lived farther along the coast from Touchstone. That might have been his car—I had only seen it in the mist and would not have recognized it again.

I started down the slope instinctively, tired of my own thoughts and aware of a desire to see him. But the car was already out of sight and a glance at my watch informed me that I was almost due at the library. Reluctantly, I turned back.

Mike was still on my mind as I took my place in the chair by Matthew's desk, and I asked idly, 'Does Mike live alone at the farm?'

Matthew looked up in surprise, and I realized that it was the first time I'd spoken to him about something other than work.

'He does now; his mother, who was my aunt, died a few months ago. But he has a housekeeper—a sister of Mrs Johnson's, actually—and the men have their own cottages scattered round the farm, so there are plenty of people about.'

'What about his father?'

'I don't remember him.'

'So he has no relatives now?'

Matthew smiled a little. 'Only me. Next question?'

I flushed. 'I'm sorry.'

'Not at all; I'm relieved to find you have a thought in your head other than your typewriter!'

Stung, I retorted, 'You don't exactly encourage conversation!'

I expected a deserved rebuke, but he merely said mildly, 'I suppose I've got out of the habit of it.'

I clenched my hands in my lap. 'Didn't you talk to Miss Harvey?'

There was a tiny silence. Then he said evenly, 'Occasionally. But we were speaking of Mike; have you seen him since you arrived?'

'Only briefly, with Sarah. Why?'

'Just that—oh, it doesn't matter.'

I said, 'He told me you don't approve of him.'

'Did he indeed?'

'Is it true?'

'Not exactly. Mike has done some pretty irresponsible things in his time, but he's always managed to get away with them. His mother idolised him—and he her. He was very cut up when she died.' He flicked an amused glance at me. 'Perhaps I should warn you that his girlfriends never last more than a week or two.'

'Really?' I said coldly.

'So don't go losing your heart to him,' he finished, only half-jokingly. 'I feel responsible for you.'

'Thank you, but I'm quite able to take care of myself.'

His eyes mocked me. 'I'm sure you are.' After a moment he went on, 'Well, if that's all you need to know about my cousin, perhaps we can continue with the book.'

I bent my head without a word and picked up my pencil. I knew he was watching me but I refused to meet his eyes again and after a brief pause he began to dictate.

As my pencil covered the pages, I was still thinking about Mike. So he'd had lots of girlfriends. Well, that was hardly surprising. I never supposed I was the first he had looked at in that dreamy, caressing way. Perhaps Linda—my thoughts skidded to a halt and my pencil faltered. Then I collected myself and the shorthand flowed smoothly on. But I had just realized that my latest attempt to speak of Linda Harvey had, as usual, been neatly parried.

* * *

The next morning dawned damp and misty and by breakfast time a heavy drizzle had started which was to persist all day.

I stood at the dining-room windows after lunch, staring through the streaming panes at the sodden garden and the outline of the gate only just visible through the rain. A free afternoon, and nothing to do. Matthew, presumably undeterred by the weather, had set off for the golf club as usual; I had seen him go, in waterproof trousers and jacket, a cap pulled over his head.

'Isn't it horrid?'

I turned to find Sarah beside me.

'And it's Saturday too!' she added disgustedly.

So it was. The days had all seemed the same since I arrived. Matthew had offered me one of my 'free evenings' the other day, but I had no plans, and since we were at an interesting point in the book, I hadn't bothered to take it. However, the thought of working on a Saturday night was not very pleasant, even if I had nothing better to do. I could at least go down to Chapelcombe to the cinema.

'And,' Sarah was continuing, 'I go back to school on Wednesday. Next year, when I'm nine, Daddy says I'll probably board.'

I must have looked surprised, because she added naively, 'I get in his way rather.'

My heart contracted. 'I'm sure you don't—he hardly ever sees you!'

'I think it's because I remind him of Mummy,' she went on, in her old-fashioned little voice. 'Not that I really *look* like her—Mummy's very beautiful—at least, I think she is—but I suppose just because I'm *here* it makes him think of her, and he doesn't like that.'

'Do you miss her, Sarah?' We were still standing at the window, and I put my arm round the thin little shoulders and pulled her against me.

'Not really. I didn't see her much, either. She was always working or at parties.'

'Working?'

'Yes, she writes, like Daddy, but on a newspaper. Tammy says she's very clever.'

My heart ached for the child, rejected by both her parents.

As though she knew what I was thinking, she looked up at me with a smile. 'I'm not lonely, though. I have Tammy—she was Mummy's nanny once—did I tell you?—and Uncle Mike is much more fun than Daddy! Daddy's always so solemn—he never laughs.'

'Perhaps he misses your mummy too.' I hadn't thought of that before.

'Yes, I suppose he does. But they always used to shout at each other when she was here, so . . .' she lifted her shoulders in an almost foreign little shrug.

I thought gratefully of my own happy family, and half-changed the subject. 'You say she's beautiful—what does she look like?'

'Would you like to see her picture?'

'Yes—yes, I would.'

'Come upstairs, then.' She tugged at my hand and I turned readily from the depressing view and went with her up the stairs and into her bedroom. It was next door to mine and roughly the same shape, decorated with a wallpaper covered in teddy bears and rabbits.

'It's a bit babyish,' Sarah apologized matter-of-factly, 'but I quite like it really.' It was uncanny how often she answered a thought in my mind.

She knelt on the floor before a little roll-top

desk and opened one of its drawers, from which she took a photograph album. She laid it on the rug in front of the gas fire. 'Let's be cosy!' she said, 'Could you light it?'

I knelt beside her on the rug, and the cheerful glow spread over us. Sarah rolled onto her stomach and opened the album at the first page. On it was pasted, somewhat crookedly, a blurred snap of a young woman in a long skirt, holding a baby. My heart sank. If this was to be the quality of the photographs, I would be no nearer knowing anything about Mrs Haig. There was a preponderance of glue, which shone dully all round the snap and even in a few spots on the print itself.

'That's Mummy and me, but you can't see it very well.' Sarah turned over. 'There!' she said triumphantly. This page was certainly more promising. There was a photo of Matthew standing with his arm round a girl. They were both laughing, and I was so surprised at this revelation of him looking young and happy, that it was a moment before my eyes passed to the figure beside him. She was attractive in a bony, long-limbed kind of way, with her hair cut in a style fashionable some years ago. Even in the snap, the lift of her chin and the stance of her body, independent of Matthew although he held her, spoke of an arrogant self-confidence. I was a little disconcerted to find that I didn't like her. No doubt I was prejudiced by what she had done to Sarah.

I glanced down at the intent little face, its usual pallor made rosy by the fire, which also woke red lights in her long, pale brown hair. For no real reason I felt tears prick my eyes. Poor, self-sufficient little Sarah. Perhaps her pathetic attempt at independence was a heritage from her mother, but she certainly had need of it.

She turned another page. 'Here's one of Uncle Mike and Auntie Laura. She was my great-aunt really.'

'Just a minute!' I held her hand as she was about to turn over again and bent to look more closely. The woman with Mike was not old, as I'd somehow expected. She was perhaps in her late forties, with a gentle, softly pretty face. Mike was standing behind her chair in an open-necked shirt. He looked much the same as he did now, so it must have been a fairly recent photograph.

'These snaps aren't in order, are they, Sarah? I mean, this wasn't taken long ago, was it?'

'I don't know, really. Mummy gave me a pile of old snaps and said I could stick them in my album. I put them in the way I wanted them.'

'Your mother gave them to you? When?'

'I don't remember.'

'But when did she go away?'

'When I was six, but she still comes to see us.'

And in between times lives it up in London,

I thought, with surprising bitterness.

'What's her name, Sarah? I mean, what name does she use for her writing? Do you know?'

'Yes, Tammy told me.' She looked up, pushing her hair back, 'Kate—and the name she had before she met Daddy—Hardacre.'

'Kate Hardacre!' I stared at her. Kate Hardacre, Sarah's mother—and Matthew's wife! I had frequently read her witty, cynical column in the Sunday papers. 'Tammy was right—she's certainly clever.'

'Do you know her?' Sarah demanded excitedly.

'I've read some of her work, and it's very good.'

She nodded, satisfied, and went on turning the pages. The snaps were nearly all of Matthew and Kate, with occasionally one of Mike. 'There aren't many of you, are there?' I remarked.

'No, they were mostly taken when Mummy and Daddy were on holiday.'

'And you weren't with them?' I shouldn't have felt surprise.

'Oh no, I was too young—I'd have been in the way,' Sarah said seriously.

My throat prickled again at this acceptance that she was nothing more than a nuisance. 'Sometime,' I said impulsively, 'you must come for a holiday with my family. We'd love to have you—we haven't any little girls.'

'Really?' She looked up, delighted.

'Really—I'll speak to Daddy about it,' I added grimly. She bent back to the book.

'Oh, here's one of Linda!'

We'd come to the last completed page of the album, and the child jumped as I snatched it up for a close look at last at the elusive Linda Harvey. The snap showed a tall, slender girl in a bikini, her blonde hair soft on her shoulders, her lips parted in a smile. She was posed on a rock, for all the world like a railway poster advertising a holiday resort. 'That's a good picture,' I said tentatively.

'Derek took it.' Her tone was dismissive.

'Who's Derek?'

'A friend of Uncle Mike's. I don't like him very much, but Linda did.'

Perhaps Derek wasn't as patient as Mike with a little girl wanting to tag along.

Sarah sat up on her heels. 'Miss Barton, did you really mean it about the holiday?'

'Of course I did. And since you called Miss Harvey Linda, don't you think you could call me Emily?'

She considered, her head on one side. 'All right, if you'd like me to.'

'Sarah—' I leaned forward urgently. 'Why did Linda—'

The sound of the opening door drowned my voice and Miss Tamworth's sharp voice said, 'Sarah, you really mustn't commandeer Miss Barton like this—she has other things to do.'

'No, really, Miss Tamworth, I was only too glad—'

'Miss Barton says I can call her "Emily",' Sarah interrupted.

'How nice,' said Miss Tamworth coldly. But there was real affection on the stern face as she looked down at the child. 'Now run along downstairs, dear. You haven't written to Mummy today, have you?'

She bent and pointedly turned off the gas fire. Then she moved across to the window and opened it wide. I stood awkwardly watching her. 'The rain's off at last,' she said, her back still to me.

I braced myself. 'Sarah showed me a photo of Linda Harvey . . .'

Her back stiffened. She said severely, 'Miss Harvey was no better than she should be!' and walked past me out of the room.

So! I pursed my lips in a soundless whistle. Was *that* why Linda had left? 'No better than she should be!' The old-fashioned phrase amused me till I started to wonder who she'd been misbehaving with. Mike? Matthew said he'd been irresponsible and got away with it—that he had plenty of girlfriends. Then, thankfully, I remembered the unknown Derek, whom Linda had liked. So *that* was all it was! I'd built up quite a mystery round Linda, and it was only Victorian prudery which made them keep changing the subject!

My heart lightened so suddenly that I was

surprised to realize how the matter must have been weighing on me, and as I stood there on the landing, the telephone shrilled in the hall below. A moment later Mrs Johnson's voice called up the stairs. 'For you, Miss Barton!'

On a wave of anticipation I sped down the curving staircase. 'Hello?'

'Emily—Mike here. I wondered if you're free this evening?'

I felt a spurt of pleasure. 'I'll have to check, but I think it'll be all right.'

'Great, I thought we'd make up a foursome with a couple of friends—go out for a meal and perhaps some dancing.'

'It sounds lovely,' I said, but I was disappointed. I didn't want to share Mike on our first date.

'I'll pick you up about seven-thirty. OK?'

'Fine—thank you.'

'Bye for now.'

'Goodbye.' As I replaced the receiver, the front door swung open with a wet, breezy rush and Matthew strode into the hall. The wet afternoon had stung colour into his face, and as he pulled off his cap, ruffling his hair in the process, he looked suddenly like the happy young man in the snapshot.

'Hello!' he said. 'You look pleased with yourself!'

'I—would it be all right if I went out this evening?'

'Ah—*hah!*' He paused in the unbuttoning of

his jacket. 'Yes, of course. But remember what I said!'

'I will,' I replied with dignity, and went back up the stairs to survey my wardrobe.

CHAPTER FOUR

By seven-thirty the mist had returned, deepening with the coming darkness. It pressed thickly against the pane of my window as I stood anxiously watching for Mike's car. Small rivulets coursed down the glass and merged with the dampness of the outside sill. It was like being imprisoned in a lighthouse, surrounded by a cold white sea.

I glanced at my watch impatiently. The mist must be holding him up. I strained my ears. Surely, above the tick of my bedside clock and the persistent drip of a tap, surely that was the sound of a car? Yes—and it had turned up off the main road—it could only be Mike.

As I watched, the mist by the gate starred into two yellow globes, and the blunt nose of the car materialized. I turned and ran out of the room and down the stairs, reaching the hall just as the front door bell pealed.

Mike stood on the step, shrouded in dampness, a scarf twisted round his neck. 'Hello, Beautiful,' he said, and before I found my voice, reached past me to close the door, took my arm, and hurried me over to the car.

'This is Emily,' he announced to two shapes in the back seat. 'Emily, meet Derek and Sandra.'

I turned obediently to look over my shoulder but could make out no features. 'Hello,' I said tentatively.

'Greetings!' responded a light male voice.

And a girl's added, 'Hi!' and giggled.

Derek! So this was Linda's old flame. He had apparently not wasted much time in seeking a replacement.

Mike climbed in beside me and slammed the door. 'Phew, what a night! At least the car's warm.'

It was the second time the car had received me in out of the fog, and the remembered smell of leather, petrol and cigarette smoke was now overlaid with the sickly sweetness of Sandra's perfume. I settled back against the seat, determined to enjoy the evening.

'Are we going to the Flamingo?' Derek enquired.

'Yes, it's as good as anywhere, isn't it? I booked a table for eight-thirty.'

Sandra said, 'I wonder if that Italian waiter is still there?' and giggled again.

Suddenly I felt left out, not one of the party. The three of them had so obviously been out together before. Who had Mike partnered then? Perhaps after all I was wrong about Derek, and it was Mike who had been with

Linda.

'How's our resident author these days, Emily?' Derek asked. 'As uproariously amusing as ever?'

Mike said with a grin, 'Matthew doesn't approve of Derek, either.'

I could understand that; although I'd not even seen his face, I knew instinctively that I disliked him.

Since they seemed to be waiting for my reply, I said awkwardly, 'He's very well—and very busy, of course.'

'But not too busy to go boozing at lunch-time and play golf all afternoon, eh?' said Derek with an unpleasant laugh.

Unwillingly I thought—so that's where he goes when we stop work at twelve. Then, defensively: And why shouldn't he? A bit of male companionship must be very refreshing, when he lived in a house full of women.

Mike shot a sideways look at me, and, noting my embarrassment, said, 'Leave her alone, Derek, it's not fair to criticize Matthew in front of her.'

Not fair to Matthew, or to me? Had Linda joined in their sneering remarks? I'd never expected to feel sorry for Matthew Haig but I did now, fleetingly—until I thought how little he would care what any of them—any of *us*—might say about him.

'Beg pardon I'm sure, miss,' Derek said. 'Didn't wish to offend, I'm sure.' And Sandra giggled again. I began to wish I had gone to the cinema after all.

The car ride seemed interminable, especially since I'd no idea where we were going. Mike gripped the wheel, eyes narrowed against the glare of the fog. Behind us, Derek and Sandra whispered and laughed softly. I sat stiff and straight, bitterly disappointed with the start of the evening to which I'd looked forward so much, while the thick whiteness enveloped us like a creeping blindness. The smell of it, cold and acrid, stung my throat and made my eyes ache.

'Well, we've made it!' Mike said at last. Ahead of us, orange lights blossomed indistinctly like sea anemonies.

'Well done, lad.' Derek removed his arm from Sandra's shoulders and got out of the car, stretching. Mike came round and opened my door. A building loomed in front of us, and Sandra and Derek, arm in arm, were hurrying towards it. He squeezed my arm reassuringly and we set off in their wake.

Pushing through the door, we emerged from the foggy darkness into a small, crowded bar.

'I'll take the coats,' Mike said, 'then fight my way to the bar. Derek, you and the girls see if you can find a table.'

'Willingly!' Derek took each of us by the arm and steered us across the room to a corner table which a couple was just leaving. His hand was hot, and gripped my bare flesh unnecessarily tightly. We sat down and he leant back in his chair and, much to my discomfort, openly studied me.

Mike inched his way over to us and set the glasses down. Derek, his eyes still on me, licked his lips with a quick, nervous movement. 'Well, well!' he said softly. 'So this is the new secretary. I must say Matthew can pick them. A pity he doesn't know what to do with them when he's got them!' He gave his light laugh. Embarrassed, I picked up my glass and twirled it in my fingers, my eyes fixed on the pale gold liquid.

I'd been right in knowing I should dislike Derek. He was good-looking in an obvious, blatantly male way, with a high colour and tight, wavy black hair. His eyes, which should also have been dark, were instead a curious yellow-hazel—like a cat's—while his lips were disturbingly sensuous, the more so from his habit of constantly licking them. The overall impression was, strangely, one of greed—a grasping, hot-breathed greed. As he turned back to Sandra I gave an involuntary shudder.

Mike's hand was warm on my arm. 'Someone walk over your grave?' he asked smilingly. I smiled back, shaking my head. 'Well now, tell me how it's going. Are you settling down all right? You mustn't let Matthew bully you, you know.'

'Everything's fine; we've established a routine now.'

He grinned at me. 'I was hoping you'd be over to see the piglets.'

I said demurely, 'Nobody invited me.'

'Well, I'm inviting you now. Any time you're free, walk over the moor to the farm. If you go on up the hill past Touchstone and follow the track you'll come to it eventually.'

'I know.'

He raised an eyebrow. 'You know?'

'I think I saw your car pass one afternoon.'

'And you didn't call? I'm hurt!'

'There wasn't time,' I murmured, remembering how I'd wanted to see him.

He frowned suddenly. 'There never is. We must make time, Emily.'

I looked at him in surprise, and he gave a short laugh. 'Time should be our servant, my sweet, not our master. Bend it to your bidding. It's later than you think, and all that jazz.' He laughed again. 'Don't look so puzzled, love, you're too serious by half!' He flicked his fingers gently against my cheek. 'Come on, drink up, it's time we went in for dinner.'

The dining-room was as crowded and hot as the bar. Our table was beside one of the long windows, curtained now against the depressing night.

'It's lovely here in summer,' Sandra said. 'The restaurant's built right out over the sea. There are tables on the balcony and you can see all the lights along the coast.'

In summer, she had said. Yes, summer was

all but over; if I wanted to get in some swimming, I couldn't afford to waste time. Following on the thought, I said, 'If it's fine tomorrow, I think I'll go down to the beach. Where's the best place to bathe?'

Sandra, who had been fiddling with a fork, dropped it with a small clatter on the table. Below the general clamour, the silence which suddenly enveloped our table was electric. I looked up, startled, and caught the warning look which flashed between the three of them. What had I said? I faltered, 'Is something wrong?'

'No, no, of course not,' Mike said quickly. 'Anywhere along the the coast is fine, provided you watch the flags. Can you—swim?'

That question again. 'Yes, quite well.'

The waiter approached with the first course, and the wave of relief was tangible. Apparently swimming was something else it was unwise to talk about. A shiver of uncertainty, almost of fear, pricked its way up my spine. What was wrong with them? Why was I shut out? Even by Mike, who'd been so gentle with me.

I don't remember much more of the evening. Afraid of saying something else wrong, I sat miserably silent, forcing down the food without tasting it. Mike exerted himself to be attentive and amusing, but I found it hard to respond. Derek and Sandra danced, their faces pressed together, their arms twined round each other. I pleaded a headache which, with the heat and blaring of the band, was almost true.

Then came the dark fog again, crouching outside the restaurant like a beast beyond the circle of the camp fire.

I shrank into my coat, turned up the collar, and clenched my hands tightly in my lap. Mike, after a glance at my face, remained silent. Behind us, subdued whispers and giggles told plainly what Sandra and Derek were up to. Well, he wouldn't ask me out again, that was for sure. A real Jonah I had turned out to be.

But it wasn't my fault! I protested silently. It was theirs, with their silences and their guarded eyes. And I couldn't help it if Derek's coarse jokes did not amuse me.

At last, the car turned into the familiar gateway and drew up in front of the house.

'Don't bother to get out,' I said quickly, seizing the handle.

'Emily—'

'Good night!' I half fell out of the car and ran quickly to the front door, where Mike caught me up.

'Emily—' he said again.

'I'm all right—please go.'

He put a finger under my chin and tilted back my head, trying to see my eyes in the light from the hall. His own were gentle, troubled, regretful. For a moment I almost wished that, disregarding my protest, he would hold me. I was in need of comfort at that moment. But he just said softly, 'I'm sorry, angel.'

'Thanks for a lovely evening!' I said in a rush, and wrenched open the front door. It closed firmly behind me, and I leant against it, blinking away tears.

Then, to my horror, I heard a door open and Matthew's voice called, 'Is that you, Miss Barton?'

Footsteps sounded from the library passage and he came round the corner into the hall. 'I was worried about the fog—' He stopped short on seeing me at bay, my back to the door. 'What is it? Whatever's wrong?' He came towards me. I levered myself away from the door with both hands, shaking my head. He said sharply, 'Did Mike—?'

'No!' I shook my head violently. 'I'm all right, really, just a—a bad headache!'

He stared at me, his eyes full of concern, and the last of my control snapped. 'Goodnight!' I choked, and, brushing past him, fled up the stairs to the sanctuary of my room.

CHAPTER FIVE

I woke slowly to the realisation that it was Sunday, the sun was shining, and that, as Mrs Johnson was at her daughter's, I would have to join the others for breakfast. I turned and buried my head in my pillow, away from the smarting sunshine. I didn't want to see anyone. Unwilling memories of the previous evening washed over me: Derek and his loose wet lips; the tension when I mentioned going swimming; and Matthew in the hall below, helplessly witnessing my distress. And I had told him I could take care of myself! What must he think of me?

Well, I thought rebelliously, sliding out of bed, they could keep their secrets, and whatever they said, I was going for a swim this afternoon. They were already in the dining-room when I went down half an hour later. Matthew nodded a greeting over his newspaper. His eyes flickered over my face, then dropped again to his reading.

'Did you have a nice time with Uncle Mike?' Sarah asked brightly.

'Yes, thank you,' I replied, pouring myself some coffee.

'Eat your breakfast, Sarah,' instructed Miss Tamworth automatically, and the moment passed.

Because Matthew was working to a deadline on the book, and Linda's departure had delayed him more than I'd realized, he'd asked earlier if I'd have any objection to working on Sundays. I hadn't, especially since I'd earn double pay; so it was agreed we'd follow the same routine as on any other day.

The novel was now progressing well, and I quite looked forward to my sessions in the library, as eager as any future reader to discover what would happen next. That morning, however, my late night and subsequent emotional upheaval weighed heavily, and it was an effort not to yawn.

After lunch I said to Sarah, 'How about coming down to the beach with me?'

'She has Sunday School this afternoon,' Miss Tamworth said primly, and not, I felt, without satisfaction. I was disappointed; Sarah was good company and I did not want to be left to my thoughts today.

However, as there was no help for it, I set off, alone as usual, down the rough road to the cliffs. Dark glasses protected my still-sensitive eyes, but even through my sandals the heat of the road scorched my feet as I crossed it. The short turf was hot and prickly, but it was springy to walk on, and a welcome breeze touched my face. Slowly in my flopping sandals I went down the worn stone steps. A smell of baking seaweed rose to meet me. The bay, as usual, was deserted. At the bottom of the steps I turned and walked along the base of the cliffs, my sandals weighted down by the hot, soft sand. I dropped the book and towel I had brought, spread out the rug, and dropped thankfully down on it.

Nothing stirred. Even the seagulls were quiet. I stripped off shirt and shorts and lay down in my swimsuit. Beneath the rug the sand shifted and moulded itself to the shape of my body. Out of the metallic blue sky the sun beat down. Orange and gold patterns flickered against my eyelids—flickered, spun and were gone. After a while I slept.

The raucous call of a gull awoke me, and I sat up, my skin feeling tight in the heat. My watch said three-thirty. It was time for that swim, and I ran down the hot sloping sand to the sea. The tepid water was cool on my hot feet and I stood for a moment, shivering deliciously as it lapped my ankles, licking away the grains of sand. Then I walked slowly forward, kicking against the water until some of the spray splashed up on my body, when, with a gasp, I plunged in.

Once under, the water was almost bath-warm. I drifted luxuriously, revelling in the gentle slap of the waves against my face, the minute rise and fall of my body supported by the sleeping sea. I floated into a patch of cold water and pushed myself lazily out of it again. A gull swooped close at hand, shearing off as I turned my head to watch it. After a while I took a breath and submerged. The water was crystal clear. A mill pond, as I had said. At the bottom, embedded in the brown sand, coloured pebbles lay like buried treasure. I remembered with a wave of nostalgia the summer holidays of long ago, when Gil had taught me to dive, and I had brought home boxes of pretty pebbles as trophies to decorate the garden.

Idly now I dived, collected a handful and came up again, treading water as I dropped back the more ordinary stones. I put my head down to watch their lazy, spinning descent. There was another batch over to my right and I set off to inspect them, swimming strongly along the bottom of the limpid water.

Just what happened next I'm still not clear. The first thing I noticed was a turmoil of water churning where all had been smooth. The next minute, to my horror, I was spun round, seized firmly by the back of my head, and dragged, struggling and coughing, up to the surface. Choking, kicking, I fought wildly to free myself, but the grip that held me was vice-like. Panic sluiced over me. Was this why I must not swim in the bay—some strange force that carried one swiftly out to sea? I opened my mouth to scream and the salt water rasped my throat.

Suddenly sand grazed my threshing legs, and I realized with a weakening flood of relief that I had been pulled not out to sea but back to the beach. Just beyond the last slow lick of water, I was abruptly dropped.

Gasping, coughing and retching, I rubbed the water out of my eyes to find myself staring unbelievingly into Matthew's white face.

'Are you all right? Oh God, Emily, I thought—'

'You!' Relief merged into indignation. 'What on earth were you doing, dragging me out like that? I was only collecting pebbles!'

He went still. 'Pebbles?'

I opened my hand. Two small shapes, smooth as birds' eggs, still lay in my palm. He stared at them in silence. Then he said expressionlessly, 'I'm sorry. You must think me a fool.'

'I *told* you I could swim.'

'I was on my way down here when I saw you go under. I didn't stop to think—I just went after you.'

Relief had made me light-headed. I said facetiously, 'Secretaries *must* be hard to find!'

He stared at me, the colour beginning to come back to his face. I shook back my dripping hair. 'Anyway, I thought you were playing golf?'

'We only had nine holes. I was hot and sticky and decided a swim would be a good idea. I don't—often come down here.'

'Well,' I said feelingly, 'it's all yours!'

He stood up abruptly. 'I seem to have lost the inclination. I'll see you at the library at five.' And with a curt nod he started back up the beach, leaving me like a stranded mermaid.

At the bottom of the steps he stooped to retrieve shirt and trousers which he had presumably flung off in his headlong dash to my rescue. I watched him all the way up the steps, but he didn't look back.

I realized that I was shivering. I got to my

feet a little shakily and made my way back to the rug, towelling myself vigorously till the nylon of my swimsuit was almost dry. Then I dug out my paperback, rolled over on my stomach and resolutely started to read.

But it was an afternoon for interruptions. I had read only the first ten pages when a shadow fell across the page. I turned and looked up, squinting into the sunshine, expecting that Matthew had changed his mind. But it was Mike who stood above me, smiling uncertainly as though unsure of his welcome. I stifled my involuntary spurt of gladness, turned back to my book, and said ungraciously, 'Oh, it's you!'

'What a welcome!' He flopped down beside me and, reaching up, twined a strand of my hair round his fingers.

I jerked my head away. 'All I wanted was a quiet afternoon,' I said crossly, 'but first Matthew comes down, and now you!'

'Matthew?' He sobered abruptly. 'Matthew was here?'

'Yes, I'm surprised you didn't meet him on the path. It was only about ten minutes ago.'

He sat up, his eyes on my damp hair. 'You went swimming together?'

'Not exactly. He charged in when I was indulging in marine studies and forcibly dragged me out.'

'Did he now?' His voice was very quiet.

I turned to look at him, puzzled. 'What's the

matter?'

There was a strange, far-away look in his eyes. Then they refocussed on me and he smiled a little. 'Nothing's the matter, honey, only—'

'Only what?'

He was silent, staring down at his hands, clasped between his raised knees. 'Only I shouldn't make a habit of swimming with Matthew, that's all.'

A little breeze sprang up from nowhere and touched my shoulders with its cool breath. I shivered.

Mike said, 'Still, don't let's waste time talking about him. I came to apologize—for last night.'

'Oh, that.' I looked away from him.

'Yes, that. I've been wondering all morning what I could say to you, but all I can come up with is—I'm sorry. Will you forgive me?'

'There's nothing to forgive.' Nothing tangible, anyway. Just the feeling of being shut out; not one of them.

'You see, Derek and I go back a long way. We've done a lot of things, been to a lot of places together. And he's been going round with Sandra for several weeks now, which is a long time for Derek! So we *know* each other, and tend to forget you don't know us too.'

He was still classing himself with them, I thought miserably.

'You forget I'm not Linda?' I said

deliberately.

'Linda?' he echoed sharply. 'What the hell?—' Then the guarded look again. 'I don't see what any of this has to do with Linda.'

'Nor do I really,' I said wearily, tired of the discussion. I liked Mike, and I didn't want to antagonise him.

I lay back on the rug and half-closed my eyes. Mike peeled off his shirt. His back was smooth and evenly-bronzed, the muscles rippling under his skin. The tiny hairs on his forearm glinted gold in the sun. Then he turned and looked down on me, his eyes gold-flecked, so wantonly long-lashed for a strong, virile man.

'Emily,' he said softly, 'forgive me, please.'

My arms lifted to receive him as his mouth came down to mine. Under my hands his back and shoulders were warm and smooth as silk. It was a wonderful kiss. At last, he raised his head far enough to meet my eyes. We smiled at each other and I sighed from sheer happiness. Coming so swiftly on my black depression, the effect was intoxicating.

He traced gently round my eyes and mouth with one finger. 'You have the most beautiful eyes, do you know that?'

With an effort I remembered Matthew's words.

'I bet you say that to all the girls!'

He smiled lazily. 'It doesn't make it any less true.'

A token denial would, I felt, have been more acceptable.

I sat up. 'I must be going. It's four-thirty and I'm due in the library at five.'

'To hell with the library,' Mike said, entirely without rancour, 'and to hell with Matthew!' He kissed me again.

All right, Matthew, I said silently, I know, I know! He's a flirt, he's had a string of girls. But after my fright in the water and Matthew's own strangeness, a little light-hearted love-making was a wonderful relief.

With an effort I pushed him away and sat up. 'Really, Mike, I must go.'

He folded the rug while I pulled on shorts and shirt. Then he slung his own shirt over one shoulder and, with his hand under my elbow, we set off up the stone steps.

At the gate of Touchstone, he handed over the rug. 'You're on your own now, sweetheart. There's an invisible notice on this gate which reads "No hawkers, vagabonds or Staceys".'

I opened my mouth to ask when I'd see him again, but prudence came to my aid. He kissed me lightly on the nose, raised a hand in salute, and continued up the sheep track to the moorland and the farm.

I turned into the drive and as I did so, caught a movement at the sitting-room window. Matthew had been watching us.

He was waiting for me in the library when I reached it, rather breathlessly, at ten past five.

‘I’m sorry I’m late,’ I murmured.

‘You’ve recovered, I see. No doubt you had more congenial company after I left.’

I did not reply.

‘Miss Barton, I might be repeating myself, but I do feel I should warn you—’

‘Not to take Mike too seriously? And if I, too, may repeat myself, I can take care of myself.’

He held my eyes for a minute, then looked irritably away. ‘As long as you know what you’re doing,’ he said shortly, and without further preamble launched straight into dictation.

As my pencil skimmed over the pages, I wondered what had caused their mutual dislike, leading each to caution me about the other—and felt a chill of apprehension before I knew why. Then I remembered that Mike’s warning had been altogether more sinister: *I shouldn’t make a habit of going swimming with Matthew.* Well, I did not intend to; my experience with him in the water was not one I wanted to repeat.

Determinedly blotting out such speculations, I forced myself to concentrate on the work in hand.

CHAPTER SIX

The sunshine was still with us the next morning, and this time my spirits were in keeping with the day. And it was Monday, I reflected as I finished my breakfast. If only all Monday mornings could be like this! It was amazing to think that this time last week, as I was driving to Paddington with Gil, I'd never even met Mike or Sarah—or Derek and Sandra.

As I came out of my bedroom, the letter-box rattled in the hall below and some envelopes fell on to the carpet. Perhaps there'd be a letter from home.

I ran downstairs and picked them up. Then I stiffened, staring down at the top envelope until the words swam into each other. Miss Linda Harvey . . .

I'm not sure why I reacted so strongly; it was quite possible that some of Linda's friends didn't know she'd left Touchstone. But I'd been hoping to see my own name, and to read hers instead was an eerie sensation. For this letter was addressed to Matthew Haig's secretary, and for a moment it was as though I, Emily Barton, did not exist—almost as though I myself were Linda Harvey.

I shook myself impatiently. Behind me, the grandfather clock struck nine, and I slipped the envelope into my pocket. Now they'd have to tell me her address, so I could forward it. I might even, I thought defiantly, deliver it personally.

The two letters addressed to Matthew I took into the library. 'The post has come, Mr Haig.'

'Thank you. I trust you slept well.' The sardonic tone was reflected in the raised eyebrow.

'Excellently, thank you.'

We started work, but I remained very conscious of Linda's letter in my pocket. Would he know her address? He must have a record of it from her original application. How long had she been here? It was ridiculous, I thought impatiently, to know so little about her. This time they would have to answer me.

The coffee came, and, half an hour later, was taken away untasted, with a reproachful look from Mrs Johnson. Matthew raced on, and my hand ached from gripping the pencil, but pride prevented me from asking him to slow down. Grimly, I concentrated on keeping up with him.

At five to twelve, he sighed and leant back in his chair. 'That was a good morning's work. Did you get it all down?'

'Yes, thank you.' I flexed my cramped fingers. Now was the moment, before he went for his pre-lunch drink. I stood up as though to return to my desk.

'Oh, Mr Haig,'—my voice was studiedly casual—'I wonder if you could let me have Miss Harvey's address?'

The effect of my words was more dramatic than I could have hoped. About to rise, Matthew halted, both hands on the arms of his chair and head lowered. Then, slowly, he sat down again and looked up at me. His eyes burned into mine. '*What* did you say?'

My mouth was suddenly dry, and I moistened my lips. 'Miss Harvey's address; could I have it, please? A—a letter has come for her.'

He let out a long-held breath. 'Well, you'd better tear it up; it won't be any use to her now.'

My eyes widened. 'I can't do that! Surely she—'

'What do you know of Linda Harvey?' he interrupted harshly. 'Who's been speaking to you about her?'

'No one, that's the point. But surely she only left because—because . . .' I stumbled to a halt.

He was staring at me, his eyes narrowed and keen as gimlets. 'Well, since you're obviously riddled with curiosity,' he said at last, with an edge to his voice, 'I might as well tell you that Linda Harvey is dead. She was drowned in the bay four weeks ago.'

Outside on the path a dog barked suddenly. From the passage I could hear Mrs Johnson busy with the vacuum cleaner. My hand went slowly to my throat as a feeling of nausea spread over me, and I remembered Matthew dragging me, kicking and struggling, out of the sea.

I whispered, 'So that was why—you thought . . .'

'Yes, that's why I dragged you so unceremoniously out of the water.' His voice was more gentle, as though he realized the shock he had given me.

'And I was flippant and silly,' I said quietly. 'I'm sorry.' What had I said? *Secretaries must be hard to find.* My face flamed.

Matthew had risen. 'I should have broken it more gently. I'm sorry. Sit down for a minute.' He went to the corner cabinet, poured a tot of what I assumed was brandy, and came back to me.

'Drink this.' I had started to shake, and he had to hold the glass for me. 'You didn't know her,' he commented, watching me curiously. 'Why has it upset you so much?'

'Because nobody told me she was dead.' I looked up at him. '*Why* didn't they?'

His eyes slid away. 'I didn't want to make an issue of it. It might have frightened you.'

'*Frightened* me?'

He made an impatient movement. 'Put you off staying, I mean.'

But Mike hadn't wanted me to know either; did *he* think I'd be frightened? And—oh God—what had he said? *Don't make a habit of swimming with Matthew.* He hadn't meant—he couldn't have meant—that was ridiculous. I forced myself to say, 'How did it happen?'

Matthew turned away and stood staring out of the window, his hands driven deep in his pockets. 'As far as we can gather, she fell asleep on a lilo and drifted out to sea. She couldn't swim.'

'How dreadful,' I whispered. 'Who—found her?'

'I did.' The tone precluded any further questioning. Poor, dead Linda. I thought of the happy girl in the snapshot and imagined her drowned beauty, blonde hair entangled with the seaweed—a floating Ophelia. I swallowed the rest of the liquid hastily and gasped as it seared my throat.

Matthew turned back to the room.

'Feeling better?'

I nodded.

'Right, then I'll go.' He could hardly leave fast enough.

But as the door closed behind him, I knew I was not sufficiently 'better' to stay alone in the room where his words still lingered. I would willingly sacrifice the afternoon to transcribe my notes, but for the moment I had to have company.

I opened the library door as the front door shut behind Matthew, waited until I heard his car start up, then walked down the passage and into the kitchen.

Mrs Johnson, busy at the sink, turned in surprise. 'Can I get you something, miss?'

'No, thank you.' I was still trembling. She dried her hands on her apron. 'What is it, miss? You look—here, sit you down by the fire.' The kitchen grate glowed cheerfully in defiance of the hot sun outside.

Gratefully I sat in the comfortable old arm chair. 'I've just heard about Miss Harvey,' I said.

'Ah. Very sad, it were. Very sad indeed. A lovely young lady.'

'Yes,' I said stupidly, hoping she would go on. That was the first unsolicited remark I'd ever heard about Linda. I put my hand in my pocket and drew out the letter. I stared at it for a moment and it shook in my hand.

'There now miss, don't 'ee fret,' Mrs Johnson said soothingly. ' 'Tis all over now, and mayhap for the best. They say her father was a parson, and a rare strict man.'

I raised my head, puzzled by the irrelevancy of the remark. 'Her father?'

'Yes. He'd never have forgiven her, likely.'

'I—don't understand.'

'I thought they told 'ee?'

'Only that—she was drowned.'

'Well now, she was expecting a baby, you see. So it would never have done.'

I'd been partly right after all. I said urgently, 'Who . . . ?'

'Why, we don't know, do we, miss? Only the

poor lady herself could have told we.'

Another thought struck me with the force of a sledgehammer. 'Then you think she—she might have . . . ?'

The woman suddenly looked frightened. 'Oh Lord love us, no, miss, that was not my meaning at all! I'm not saying as how the poor young lady did anything a-*purpose*! Such a happy creature she was, right up to the end. No thought of drowning herself, I'd stake my life. Dear me no!'

The good soul looked horrified and I abandoned the supposition stillborn. Nevertheless, that would have been a more feasible reason for not telling me and there was, after all, someone besides Linda who knew who the father was.

Slowly I leant forward and tossed the unopened envelope into the heart of the fire. It browned at the edges like an autumn leaf, darkened, slowly curled, flamed briefly, became transparent. And still the cramped handwriting was weirdly legible, like a letter to a ghost. Mrs Johnson moved to the fire and the breeze of her movement wafted it up the wide chimney. Perhaps Linda would get her letter after all.

I shivered, and Mrs Johnson clucked sympathetically. 'Not a nice thing to hear, miss; I'm surprised Mr Haig told you. I was ordered very particular not to mention Miss Linda, which was why I was a mite startled when you spoke of her that morning.'

'Why?' I asked sharply. 'Why wasn't I to be told?'

'Well,' Mrs Johnson replied with logic, 'mayhap he foresaw how the news would affect 'ee.'

'One last thing, Mrs Johnson. There was an inquest, I suppose?'

'Yes, indeed, a nasty affair. Poor Mr Haig was in a fair pother.'

'And—what was the verdict?'

'Why, death by misadventure, miss, what else?' Mrs Johnson replied serenely.

* * *

The Monday which had dawned so brightly was spoilt for me, and even Mike's phone-call at lunch time did not lift my sense of depression.

'How's my girl today?'

'So-so.' I kept my voice low and my eyes on the dining-room door, through which I had hurried to take the call.

'What's wrong, honey?'

'I've just heard about Linda.'

There was a silence. Then he said, 'What have you heard?'

'I can hardly tell you over the phone.'

'Look, I was ringing to say I'm tied up today, and how about tomorrow? But if you're upset, I could manage half an hour around four o'clock. How would that be?'

'Oh Mike, could you? I've some typing to do first, but if we could have a cup of tea together . . .'

'Right. Try not to worry, and I'll call for you at four.'

I was waiting at the gate when he drove up. The dear old car had been standing in the sunshine, and as I leant back in the seat the warm leather came round my shoulders like an embrace.

Mike leaned over and kissed my cheek. 'There's a café in town I use sometimes. Shouldn't be too busy on a Monday—we can talk there.' He was more serious than I'd seen him, and I was glad. I was not in the mood for flirting today.

The Tudor Café was oak-beamed, with shining brass and copper, and delph racks on the wall. Mike led me down the length of it to the table by the wide brick fireplace, now screened with an arrangement of chrysanthemums and dahlias. Their bitter-sweet perfume overlaid the scent of floor polish and hot buttered toast. There were only one or two people there, all at the other end of the room.

'Now.' Mike settled forward, his arms on the table. 'Who exactly told you what?'

Falteringly, I repeated the events of the morning. 'It's true, isn't it?'

'As far as it goes, I suppose.'

'Mike—' I clenched my hands. I had to ask this. 'What did you mean about not making a habit of swimming with Matthew?'

He frowned. 'I shouldn't have said that.'

'But what did you mean?'

He shrugged. 'Only that he wasn't much help to Linda.'

'I don't understand.'

'He was with her that afternoon. Didn't he tell you that bit?'

I went cold. 'He told me he had *found* her.'

'That too—later. Of course, at the inquest he said he'd left her half an hour earlier.'

'And you didn't believe him?' My palms were clammy with sweat.

'I don't know what to believe. No doubt he'd have saved her if he could.'

We were silent while the waitress brought the tea. Automatically, I poured it.

'Mike . . .' I stumbled to a halt, my face burning.

'About the baby?' he said quietly. 'It wasn't mine, Emily.'

I let out my breath on a sigh, not looking at him. 'I'm sorry.'

He laid his hand over mine. 'She was Derek's girl, and it's my guess he was the one, but you never know. Does it matter?'

I knew that it shouldn't, but it did. I was greatly relieved Mike wasn't the father, but I found that I didn't want it to be Matthew, either.

As though reading my thoughts, he added, 'She had a soft spot for Matthew, mind you. Sorry for him, I suppose—wanted to mother him.'

'Why did his marriage go wrong?' I asked curiously, ready, now, to drop the subject of Linda.

'It was always the attraction of opposites; Kate's a social animal, better suited to the bright lights, but Matthew wouldn't leave Cornwall. So the house was always full of people—parties, weekend guests—they were never alone together. Eventually she just upped and left him, but it's my belief he'd have her back any time. They rowed like hell the whole time, but he was knocked for six when she went. We—my mother and I—saw a lot of him at that time, and the stuffing just seemed to go out of him. It's taken him a long time to get back more or less to normal.'

'Poor Matthew,' I said softly. 'And poor Sarah, too.'

'Yes, she's a nice little thing. Loves to come to the farm and watch the animals being fed. I bring her here sometimes for an ice-cream.' He patted my hand. 'Don't fret about her, honey. Kate wasn't much cop as a mother, and she gets love of a sort from old Tammy.'

He grinned suddenly. 'The old battle-axe couldn't abide Linda! Came upon her and Derek once in what are known as compromising circumstances. She was outraged.'

'I can imagine,' I said. So we were back to Linda again. Well, her ghost was surely laid and I could now forget her. And for what it was worth, if Matthew was still in love with his wife, he was unlikely to have been Linda's lover. I was surprised how little comfort there was in the thought.

Mike glanced at his watch. 'Now, Cinderella, we'd better be going. I've a man coming to see me about some poultry feed at five.'

'Thanks for meeting me, Mike. I needed to talk to someone.'

'A pleasure, always!'

We drove back in silence, and again he stopped outside the gates. He kissed me on the mouth.

'Don't worry your pretty head about the past, my love. The future's all that matters. See you tomorrow?'

'Fine. What shall we do?'

'How about dinner at the farm—you've not been there yet. Derek and Sandra are coming too.'

My precarious happiness faded and my face must have shown it.

Mike said a trifle impatiently, 'Look, Emily, they're my friends. Try to like them.' It sounded to me like an ultimatum—like them, or you kiss me goodbye. And I didn't want to do that. They'd a longer-standing claim on him than I had, I reminded myself, and if I wouldn't play ball on his terms, there were plenty of girls who would.

CHAPTER SEVEN

As I dressed for my date with Mike the next evening, I was determined to be good company. I would not let Derek's suggestiveness or Sandra's inanity get under my skin as I had on Saturday. Mike was worth the effort of being pleasant to his friends, whatever my private opinion of them.

I opened my bedroom door to come face to face with Matthew, on his way upstairs. His eyes took in the new lilac dress.

'Mike again?'

'Mike again.'

'Well, enjoy yourself. You make me feel old!' He nodded and went along the passage to his room.

This time, Mike was alone when he called for me.

'The others will be along later—they're calling at the pub for a crate of beer.' His eyes went over me, warm, personal and admiring—quite different from Matthew's non-committal gaze. 'You look good enough to eat!'

We drove down to the main road and turned left, away from the town. The road hugged the coast for a while and I guessed we must have come this way through the fog to the Flamingo. Now, it was a calm September evening, the sky washed with deep blue, pink and gold as though splashed by a careless paint brush. Tiny fragments of cloud trailed like purple chiffon, and the seagulls, soaring into the sunset, became birds of flame. I drew a deep breath. It was all so perfect that it hurt.

After a while the road left the coast to turn inland, passing scattered cottages and farms until we branched off it altogether up a steep, twisting lane with high hedges on either side. A wooden post announced 'Chapel Farm. Private Road.'

'Very imposing!' I said.

'We have to keep the rabble out!' He drew up in front of a white, five-barred gate.

'I'll open it,' I said, and slipped out of the car. The gate swung easily and Mike edged the car through. We were in the farmyard, and I gave an involuntary exclamation of delight.

The farm buildings and the long, low house formed three sides of a square, all of them painted white, and glowing in the setting sun. In the centre of the yard was a patch of grass, smooth and emerald green, with a copper beech tree in the middle of it.

'Oh Mike!'

He got out of the car and came to join me. I could see he was pleased by my delight. 'Yes, it is rather fine. Those are the byres and stables over there, and opposite us the pig and poultry sheds. This gate leads to the men's cottages behind the farm house. It's quite a little colony, as you can see.'

'It's lovely, and so spotless!' True enough, the cobbles underfoot looked as though they'd been scrubbed.

'"Seven maids with seven mops"!' Mike laughed, taking my arm. 'Come inside and meet Mrs Trehearn. Since you're "company" we'll use the front door.'

We went through the low entrance into a tiny flagged passage. There was an oak door on either side and one straight ahead. Mike flung this open and I found myself in a real, old-fashioned farm kitchen, complete with an enormous white-scrubbed table and a huge open grate.

A small, thin woman came forward to greet us, nodding her head and watching me with tiny bright eyes. So this was Mrs Johnson's sister.

'How do you do, miss, I heard from Patsy as you'm come.'

'How do you do?' I turned back to Mike, who was smilingly watching my reactions.

'Come through to the sitting-room and I'll get you a drink.'

We went back down the passage and he opened one of the other doors. This opened into a long, low-ceilinged room prettily decorated in blue and white. The chairs and sofa were floral patterned, and there were some Dresden figures on the mantlepiece. Above the fireplace, dominating the room, was a large portrait of a young girl. Mike noticed my eyes on it. 'That's my mother,' he said.

'She was lovely.'

He stood for a long moment, his eyes on the painting, and I remembered Matthew saying how upset he'd been at her death. To distract him, I went on, 'And what a lovely room—not quite what you'd expect in a farmhouse!'

He nodded and, as I'd hoped, turned away from the portrait.

'Yes, I love the place, even if we haven't been here for generations, like the Haigs at Touchstone. It was actually bought for my uncle, Grandfather's younger son, but he was killed by a tractor soon afterwards. So when—my father died, Mother moved here with me.'

He laughed. 'A Grace and Favour residence, as you might say! Fortunately, we have a marvellous bailiff: Simkins. He's virtually run the farm for over twenty years.'

The sun was off the windows now and an autumn coolness breathed through the room. I walked to the log fire and sniffed appreciatively.

'Apple wood,' Mike said.

'Isn't it rather lonely out here,' I asked, 'with only Mrs Trehearn for company?'

'She doesn't live in, either. Her husband's my head cowman—they live in one of the cottages at the back. No,' he went on reflectively, 'I can't say I'm ever lonely.' He grinned, sliding an arm round my waist. 'I can usually find company when I want it!'

'But seriously, Mike, I should have thought Matthew would have invited you to Touchstone more often. After all—'

He dropped his arm and turned away. 'I don't want Matthew's company any more than he wants mine.'

'But *why*?' I asked helplessly.

The door-bell rang, and Mrs Trehearn's footsteps sounded in the passage as she went to answer it.

'Mike?' I insisted, laying a hand on his arm. He paused and looked down at me, an odd expression in his eyes. 'There are some things I can't forgive Matthew, Emily, but you needn't concern yourself with them. Drink your sherry, there's a good girl, and stop asking questions.'

There were voices in the hall, and as Mike opened the door, Derek staggered in with the crate of beer, Sandra behind him.

Mike helped him to lay the crate in a corner. Derek straightened. 'Phew—it'll be easier carrying that outside than in!' He bowed to me. 'Good evening.'

I wondered if they were as disappointed to see me as I them. They probably feared I would cast a dampener on their evening again.

I made a conscious effort. 'Come and get warm,' I said to Sandra, and she moved over to join me at the fire. She was quite beautiful with her silver blonde hair hanging like a pale curtain and her wide, china-blue eyes—not, I thought suddenly, unlike Linda. But there had been animation on the face in Sarah's album, whereas Sandra's, perfect and heart-shaped though it was, was almost doll-like in its lack of expression.

'Time for a quick one before we eat,' Mike said, handing glasses to the new arrivals. 'Want yours topping up, Emily?'

I was about to refuse when it occurred to me that an extra mouthful of sherry might help me into the party mood, and I held out my glass.

'And how's Emily tonight?' inquired Derek jovially, standing with his back to the fire and rocking backwards and forwards on his heels.

'Very well, thank you.'

'Making the most of the sunshine, I see.' His eyes rested on my brown neck and shoulders and I felt uncomfortable.

'I have to keep out of it.' Sandra said complacently, 'or I *scorch*, with my skin being so fair.'

'Give me the nut-brown maiden,' murmured Derek in an undertone, as she turned to speak to Mike.

Mrs Trehearn knocked on the door. 'The meal's ready when you are, sir.'

'Right, thank you, we'll go straight in.'

I moved forward quickly, noticing from the

corner of my eye that Derek's hand was coming up to take my arm. I remembered all too well the unpleasant warmth of his fingers, and wondered how Sandra could bear to let him touch her.

The dining-room was tiny—barely enough space for the table and four spindly-legged chairs. A huge copper plate hung on one wall and a gas fire glowed on another.

The meal was simple, but beautifully cooked. Succulent roast shoulder of lamb followed a clear soup, and we finished with apple pie and thick yellow cream.

'I pity the girl who marries Mike,' Derek said, with a sly look at me. 'She's a lot to live up to!'

Mike said, 'Mrs Trehearn's a wonderful cook, but she has her limitations in other ways!'

Derek laughed loudly and banged his hand down on the table, setting the glasses tinkling.

The meal finished, we returned to the sitting-room. Mike threw another log on the fire, and we settled round it.

After a while Mrs Trehearn knocked on the door. 'I'm going now, sir, if there's nothing else you want. Nice to have met you, miss. Goodnight, all.'

We complimented her on the meal and she beamed with pleasure. 'See you in the morning, sir,' and she was gone.

Mike put on another record. The meal and

the warmth made me sleepy. I leant back and closed my eyes, opening them after a moment to find Derek watching me. The firelight flickered grotesquely on his face, liquefying his eyes to molten gold and glinting redly on his black hair. He looked like a harbinger of hell at some obscene ritual. I stirred uneasily. Across the room, Mike said, 'Damn, I can't find the opener.'

'It's on the kitchen table,' I said. 'I'll get it.'

Glad to escape from Derek's gaze, I slipped out of the room and down the short passage into the kitchen. The big room was full of shadows, lit only faintly by the now-dying fire. A memory of the roast lamb hung on the air. I fumbled round the wall for the light switch but couldn't find it. Then I saw the bottle-opener glinting in the light from the passage. I moved forward, and as I reached for it the light was blotted out by a figure in the doorway. I turned, startled, and two hands gripped my shoulders.

Derek's voice said breathlessly, 'Let's look for it together.'

'I've got it!' I said shrilly. 'Please let go, you're hurting me.'

He laughed excitedly and his mouth, open and searching, fastened on mine. I pummelled frantically against his chest with clenched fists, and his teeth bit into my lip as he pressed himself against me.

With both hands I wrenched his face to one

side, opened my mouth to scream, and found despairingly that I had no breath. 'Mike!' It was little more than a gasp.

Derek was breathing fast. 'Playing hard to get, sweetheart?'

'You're disgusting!' I half-sobbed, forgetting my resolution. *'No!'* This as his head turned and his mouth moved over my face again. Instinctively I jerked away and as I did so, ground my high heel with all my strength into his foot. He let me go then, swearing fluently, and in that moment the room flooded with light and Mike stood in the doorway. I staggered back against the table for support, scrubbing the back of my hand against my mouth.

'I thought you were going to the bathroom,' he said tightly to Derek.

'So I was, but Emily in the dark was more than I could resist. Quite a little spitfire, isn't she? You're a lucky fellow.'

'Leave her alone, Derek, do you hear me?' Mike's voice was low and vibrant.

'But my dear chap, we're friends, aren't we? All that I have is yours, and so on. I'm sure Sandra—'

'Shut up! Are you all right, Emily?'

'I don't know.' I was fighting down the urge to retch.

'Of course she's all right, silly little bitch. She hasn't been raped, for God's sake. Calm down, Mike. I was under the impression that we shared *everything*?'

Suddenly the look he shot at Mike was no longer playful, and incredibly, Mike's own furious gaze faltered. I thought, in bewilderment, he can't be *afraid* of Derek? But his unexpected withdrawal from the challenge reflected on me, making me feel cheapened.

When Mike remained silent, Derek laughed softly and straightened his jacket. 'That's better,' he said pleasantly. 'Well, I think you'd better take Priscilla Prune home, before we offend her modesty any further. I'll amuse myself with Sandra till you get back. Pity *she* doesn't protest occasionally; it would add a touch of piquancy.'

He sauntered past us and out of the room. Mike and I stood looking at each other. I could taste the blood on my lip.

I said shakily, 'If my brother had been here, he'd have knocked him down.'

'I'm not your brother.'

'Mike, he—he—' I choked to a stop.

'Yes, I know, but he didn't mean any harm. Derek considers any girl fair game. Most of them like it.'

'Well, I don't,' I said violently.

'Emily, I'm sorry, what more can I say? Get your stole and I'll take you home.'

We drove back once more in silence, and I remembered my optimism on the outward journey. Up, down—up, down, like a yoyo.

How could Mike possibly feel friendship for anyone as objectionable as Derek? Yet he'd made only a token protest on my behalf, and withdrawn even that.

He stopped the car at the gate and came with me up the path. At the door he kissed his fingers and laid them very gently on my swollen lips. 'Goodnight, love. Try to forget it.'

Miserably, I went into the house.

* * *

When I came down the next morning, Sarah was standing in the hall in her school uniform. She looked rather forlorn under the large hat, reminding me of my own desolation at the beginning of term.

Matthew came down the stairs behind me. 'Back to school, eh? Well, the summer's over.'

'I'd forgotten it was today,' I said, smiling at her. 'I'll miss you!' The mid-day meal would be bleak without her chatter.

She gave me a tremulous smile and her eyes slid to Matthew for a word of encouragement. But he had already turned away and was leafing through the morning mail. It seemed he could never spare her more than a minute of his time.

On an impulse I bent and kissed her. 'Tell me all about it this evening.'

Miss Tamworth approached, drawing on her gloves. 'Ready, Sarah? We must leave now or we'll miss the bus.'

'Yes, I'm ready.' The child gave another hopeless little glance at her father's back, then walked silently past him following Miss Tamworth out of the front door.

My heart ached for her, but—perhaps fortunately—before I could make any comment, Matthew said brusquely, 'What happened to your lip?'

The colour washed up my face in an embarrassing flood. Despite my care with my lipstick, the deep cut, I knew, was clearly visible. 'Nothing,' I muttered with bent head.

He said drily, 'You always return from your evenings with my cousin somewhat the worse for wear.'

That brought my head up. 'It was nothing to do with Mike!'

He raised an eyebrow. 'Forgive me. I was under the impression that if you went out with a man, you stayed with him all evening.'

I twisted my hands helplessly and his voice hardened.

'Was it that Derek chap?'

Miserably I nodded.

'I might have guessed. God knows what Mike sees in him. I hope he got what he deserved.'

I made no comment.

Matthew gave a short laugh. 'Sorry, I'm not trying to embarrass you. Come on, let's get to work.'

He gestured me ahead of him. 'All the same,' he added, closing the library door behind us, 'I shouldn't have too much to do with Derek. He's an unsavoury piece of work.'

'It's not from choice; he just always seems to be there.'

'Then tell Mike you'd prefer him not to be.' Matthew's voice was brisk. He settled himself at his desk.

'I tried,' I persisted, wanting, now we had got this far, to put my case. 'But Mike won't hear anything against him.'

Matthew looked at me reflectively. 'Look, you've only been here a week. Don't be in too much of a hurry to fall for Mike.'

I said curiously, 'What is it you've got against him?'

He frowned. 'Nothing really—nothing concrete. It's just that he's changed completely since his mother died. When she was alive they were often round here—after all, we were more or less brought up as brothers. He was always a bit wild but he was good company and we got along fine. When my aunt died, I thought we'd be closer than ever. I'd hoped to help him over the worst of it, as they'd—' he broke off, then went on, 'as they'd helped me in the past.'

When Kate left, I thought.

'But quite suddenly he wouldn't have anything to do with me. For months he was a bag of nerves and would see no one but that confounded Derek.'

He lit a cigarette and tossed the still-smoking match into the waste-paper basket. 'He's better than he was, but that evening he brought you from the station was the first time I'd seen him in weeks.' He straightened. 'Anyway, that's enough about Mike. Have you got your notebook?'

We worked steadily through the morning and at about twelve he closed the file of notes. 'By the way, I'd like you to ring up a Mrs Statton and ask if it would be convenient for us to call and see her sometime this week. The number's here.'

My curiosity must have shown, because he said shortly, 'She's the housekeeper.'

'The housekeeper?' My voice was blank.

Matthew said impatiently, 'Yes, the murdered man's.' My eyes widened and he gave a short laugh. 'My mistake—didn't I explain? The book's loosely based on fact; the murder took place as I was about to start a new novel, and being local it interested me, specially as they still haven't found the culprit. But I used only the bare outline, and of course none of the characters are based on real people. In fact, all I know of the actual case is what I read in the papers or Mrs Statton told me.'

He pulled open a desk drawer, flicked through a folder and handed me a torn piece of newspaper, dated four months previously.

'Here.'

> *'Well-known artist found dead,'* I read. *'Cameron Menzies, the Royal Academician, was found murdered in his luxury flat this morning. He is believed to have been struck from behind. His housekeeper, Mrs Amy Statton . . .'*

'I was intrigued by the apparent lack of motive,' Matthew explained, as I looked up. 'Nothing was stolen from the flat, and there were plenty of valuable things there. And without a motive, it's extremely difficult to find the murderer. So I selected some of the most common, invented a character that each could apply to, and decided to write the book from several angles and see which was the most convincing.'

I shuddered. 'It's a bit gruesome, when you think of it like that.'

'Murder usually is,' Matthew said drily. 'Well, we'll see if Mrs Statton has anything new to say. In any case, I want to refresh my memory on a couple of points. Let me know at lunch-time what you've been able to arrange.'

* * *

I made an appointment with Mrs Statton for Friday afternoon, then hung around the house for a while. I was half-expecting Mike to ring, but he didn't. Perhaps he preferred not to make a habit of phoning after each date, to apologize for the previous evening. In any event, I had to admit I was disappointed in him after his attitude towards Derek. It was, I felt, carrying friendship a little too far.

Disconsolately I gathered rug and books and made my way down to the cove. But although the sun kept promising to come through it never actually emerged, and a cool little breeze ensured that I kept my jacket round my shoulders. After a while my eyes wandered from the page of my book, and I sat gazing out over the pale water which mirrored the cloud-flecked sky, wondering if Linda had sat here with Matthew the afternoon she died. I was filled with an aching sense of melancholy. I had missed Sarah at lunch. The first phase of my stay at Touchstone had ended. Matthew had said, 'Summer is over,' but I passionately wanted to hold on to it.

I'd had enough of my broodings by three-thirty and made my way back up the steps. Half way up, a grass track branched off and meandered away round the cliff face. I paused, wondering whether to follow it, but the freshness of the breeze up here was cool through my thin clothes and I decided not to bother.

As I crossed the grass towards the main road, the hourly bus lumbered up the hill from the town and stopped opposite the road leading to Touchstone. Sarah clambered down, clutching her hat and satchel. She saw me and waved and I went to meet her.

'You *are* lucky, spending the afternoon on the beach!' she greeted me.

I felt better already for seeing her. 'It wasn't very pleasant as a matter of fact; it was windy and the sand kept blowing in my face.'

She slipped her hand into mine and my fingers closed round it. 'How was school?'

'Oh, stuffy! We've got three new girls in our class.'

'But you do enjoy it, don't you?'

'I suppose so. Yes, it's good fun really, and the summer holidays *are* rather long, when you've no one to play with.'

'Don't any of your schoolfriends come over?'

'Not often. We can't play in the garden because we disturb Daddy, and we're not allowed on the beach unless Tammy goes with us, and she hates it.' She skipped a few steps. 'Do you like working for Daddy?'

I was taken aback. 'Well, yes—it's very interesting.'

'He laughs more, since you came,' she said surprisingly.

'I can't say I've noticed,' I replied as we turned into the gateway. Miss Tamworth was standing at the door.

'Hello, dear. Change out of your uniform and you may play for half an hour before tea.'

'Get a ball and I'll play with you,' I said impulsively. 'We shan't disturb your father because he won't be working until five.'

'Oh, goodie!' Sarah ran upstairs, unfastening her blouse as she went. Without comment Miss Tamworth followed her. I dropped my rug and book on the hall chair and went outside again.

I really enjoyed the next half hour. Under Sarah's instructions I recalled the games I had played at her age—French skipping, a primitive hop-scotch with sticks laid on the grass, and a multitude of ball games. We were both laughing and out of breath when Miss Tamworth called Sarah in to tea.

'That was super, Emily!' She tucked her warm, dirty little hand in mine. 'Can we play again tomorrow?'

'I don't see why not.'

We went into the hall just as Matthew appeared from the library passage.

'Daddy, Emily's been playing with me in the garden!'

'So I saw.'

'I hope we didn't disturb you,' I faltered. 'I thought you were out.'

'Daddy, we've three new girls in—'

'Not now, Sarah. Have you no homework to do?'

The light went out of her face and instinctively my arm went round her. 'Not tonight,' she replied with bent head.

I glared at Matthew but he turned away. 'Very well. I believe Miss Tamworth said your tea was ready.'

'Yes.' She looked up at me with a little smile. 'Thanks for the game, Emily.' And she walked slowly and unchildishly to the cloakroom to wash her hands.

I took a deep breath. The hall clock chimed the quarter short of five. Matthew's eyes rested on it meditatively. I took the hint. Gathering up my rug and book from the chair where I'd thrown them, I walked up the stairs with as much dignity as my short beach dress would allow.

CHAPTER EIGHT

When we set out after an early lunch on Friday, there had still been no word from Mike. Matthew had not mentioned him again, though I'd caught him watching me speculatively once or twice as I involuntarily raised my head when the phone rang. Perhaps he was afraid I'd go the same way as Linda, I thought with grim humour, and then remembered where Linda's way had led her.

It was a wet, depressing day. A windy night had loosened the leaves, which drifted disconsolately down on to the sodden grass. I settled myself back in the seat and prepared to make the most of the few hours away from my desk. Matthew's car was very different from Mike's. Smooth red leather upholstery and a radio ensured that the journey, despite the weather, would be as pleasant as possible.

'Comfortable?' he enquired, as we swooped down the hill into Chapelcombe.

'Very, thank you.' The lighted shop windows threw pools of gold on to the glistening pavements and shoppers scurried from one doorway to the next under large umbrellas, for all the world like a race of animated mushrooms. The wet tyres keened pleasantly on the surface of the road. I sat contentedly watching Matthew's strong hands resting on the wheel and the rhythmic arc of the windscreen wipers.

'Are you happy at Touchstone, Emily?'

The question, no less than the Christian name, took me by surprise, breaking in on my reverie. I glanced at him, but his eyes were on the road. 'Yes, thank you,' I stammered, and wondered, even as I spoke, if it were the truth. My emotions since reaching Cornwall had been more violent and more diverse than I had ever known them. One moment I was supremely happy, the next in the depths of despair. I tried to analyze them: I was uncertain of Mike, detested Derek, enjoyed my work. In addition, the story of Linda's death had upset me, and I was worried about Sarah's loneliness; conflicting emotions which did not add up to unclouded joy.

'You think you can put up with us till the book's finished?'

So that was all that was worrying him! I said stiffly, 'I'll keep to my contract, Mr Haig.'

Out on the open road the wind buffeted the car, flinging handfuls of hard rain against the windows. Our moving cabin was the only warmth and dryness in all the torrential afternoon. Heavy clouds obscured the sea and blotted out the moorland over which we skimmed. A scattered string of houses, squat and grey in the rain, rushed to meet us, heralding the approach of another town. Matthew sped through the empty streets with scarcely diminished speed. He did not speak again until we were once more in open countryside.

'Have you been away from home before?'

Another unexpected question. 'No.'

'You're not homesick?'

'I don't think so.'

'You'd know if you were. It's one of the most wretched conditions in the world.'

'You speak from experience?'

'Yes; I was sent to boarding-school at the tender age of seven.'

'Yet you're intending to send Sarah?' I couldn't help myself. I knew as soon as I'd spoken he would resent the implied criticism, and noticed with foreboding the tightening of his hands on the driving-wheel.

'It teaches a child independence,' he said abruptly. After a moment he added, almost as though hoping for my agreement, 'And Touchstone is no place for a child. She'd be happier at school.'

With an effort I kept quiet. It was no business of mine, after all. But I remembered how the light went out of her face every time her father turned away.

'Have you any brothers or sisters?'

Quite a catechism, this! 'One brother. He works in the City.'

'And your parents are both alive?'

'Yes.' My tone was one of patient resignation. It was unintentional, but he heard it.

'Unless we're to drive along in total silence, it seems I must make conversation. If it annoys you, I'll switch on the radio instead.'

I flushed. 'I'm sorry. It doesn't annoy me.'

'Good,' he said caustically. 'Anyway, we're nearly there.'

I looked out of the window again. We were now in the suburbs of a fairly large town, and austere grey houses lined the road in dignified rows. There was a church, a parade of shops. Matthew turned right at some traffic lights, right again, and we were in a street of smaller, terraced houses, with neat front gardens and net curtains at the windows.

'Number fifty-two,' he murmured. 'I think it's just beyond this lamp post. Yes, here we are.' He drew in to the curb and switched off the engine. In the sudden silence the rain pattered loudly on the roof of the car. 'Did you bring an umbrella?'

'No, but it doesn't matter.' I turned up the collar of my macintosh.

Matthew got out and came round to open my door. Together we hurried up the short path.

The front door opened as we reached it to reveal an elderly lady in a mauve cardigan. 'Good afternoon, sir. What a day you've brought with you!'

We surrendered our dripping macs in the tiny hall and went through the door indicated into the small front room. A fire burned cheerily in the grate, winking on the brass fender and coal scuttle. Above the fireplace was a small painting of a fishing village, and in front of it, completing the homely comfort, a black cat stretched luxuriously.

On a low table a bowl of autumn crocuses speared the shadowed corner with their purple flame, and beside them lay a tray ready laid for afternoon tea.

'Mrs Statton, may I introduce my secretary, Miss Barton?'

I held out my hand and noticed the surprise with which she took it as she looked at me for the first time. 'Oh,' she said, 'you're not the young lady who came before. I thought—'

Matthew said, 'Miss Harvey isn't with me

any more,' and I wondered if only I heard the rough edge to his voice.

I said quickly, 'I was just admiring your painting, Mrs Statton. Is it an original?'

Her face lit with pride. 'Yes, Miss, Mr Menzies gave me that hisself. He used to tease me about it. "Sell it, Mrs Statton," he'd say, "and it will keep you in your old age!" Not that I ever would.'

'Did he sign it?' I bent closer, peering through the masterful brush strokes to discern a signature.

She smiled. 'That he did. Look.' Her horny finger reached past me and pointed to a tiny thistle in the bottom left-hand corner. 'That's how he signed all his paintings, miss. His little affectation, he called it.' She smiled fondly at the painting, then turned back to Matthew, who had been quietly listening. 'Now, sir, before we start our chat I'm sure you and the young lady could do with a nice hot cup of tea to warm you up. The kettle's on, if you'll excuse me.'

She bustled from the room, and I sat down in the chair she had indicated. 'I hadn't realized you'd brought Linda here.'

'Of course I brought her; what's a secretary for?'

I bit my lip. He lit a cigarette and the spurt of the match illumined the planes of his face—the grooves from nose to mouth, the lines at the corner of his eyes. Not a happy face, I thought suddenly. How would he have replied if I'd parried his own question back at him?

He inhaled deeply and tossed the spent match into the fire. A coal shifted and the cat lazily stretched its paws, claws outspread. Its fur glistened redly in the firelight, reminding me unpleasantly of Derek. I was still watching it when Mrs Statton came back with the squat brown teapot.

'Now,' she said comfortably as she began to pour, 'how can I help you, sir?'

I declined her offer of a scone and opened my notebook. Matthew, unhampered by a pencil, bit appreciatively into one. 'You remember, Mrs Statton, that this is all unofficial—purely for my own interest?'

'Oh yes, sir, you explained last time. It's exciting, helping with one of your books, though I'm sorry it's on account of poor Mr Menzies.'

'I know it's a bore, but could you possibly run through it all again? There are some points I'd like to check, and Miss Barton, hearing it for the first time, might notice something which has escaped us. As you know, being a writer and not a policeman, I'm as interested in who might have done the murder, as in who actually did.'

'Well, as to that sir, I couldn't say, I'm sure. Whoever could have wanted to do such a thing? Such a nice gentleman he was, not like some of them painters nowadays.'

'Let's recap, then,' Matthew said. 'Mr Menzies was a widower, wasn't he?'

'That's right. His wife died five years ago, just before Miss Lesley's wedding.'

'He got on well with his daughter?'

'Apple of his eye, she was. Living in London when all this happened.'

'You didn't live in the apartment yourself, did you?'

'No, sir. I used to arrive at eight-thirty each morning—had my own key—and take Mr Menzies a cup of tea. I'd do the house over, and shop, cook his dinner, and leave soon after six in the evening.'

'A long day,' Matthew commented.

'But I enjoyed it. There was no one needing me here.'

'And on the day in question?'

Mrs Statton braced herself. 'Well, sir, it was just like any other day. I cooked his dinner for him—he liked his main meal at midday. In the afternoon I did a little mending and Mr Menzies read. Great reader, he was.'

'He didn't seem any different—worried about anything?'

'Bless you no, sir. If he had, I'd have remembered later—after it all happened.'

'So there was nothing unusual?'

She shook her head.

I glanced at Matthew, thinking of the novel. As he'd said, the characters in it were very different from real life—the importunate friend, the spendthrift nephew, the calculating brother. *No resemblance to any living person,* I thought wryly.

He leant forward and placed his cup and saucer on the table. 'Now Mrs Statton, I know this upsets you, but we'll be as quick as we can—'

'Yes, sir. Well, as I was leaving, I spoke to Dawson in the hall—'

'Ah yes, the porter. I'd forgotten that.'

'—and he said as how there was to be a big party that evening at number thirty-four. Rather cross, he was, because there would be a lot of noise, and complaints from the other residents, and all.'

'Which was why,' Matthew said slowly, 'among so many strangers in the building that night, the murderer was able to slip in without being noticed.'

'Yes, sir.' She twisted a handkerchief in her hands and kept her eyes on it. 'Well then, the next morning I arrived at half-past eight as usual. First thing I noticed was all the lights was on. I called, I think—then I pushed open the sitting-room door.'

There was a short silence, punctuated only by the unconcerned ticking of the clock and the deep-throated purr of the cat on the rug.

'And—there he was, sir. Lying on his face, with his head—'

'Yes, all right,' Matthew said quickly, and Mrs Statton drew a long, steadying breath.

'I'm all right, sir. There was this heavy vase lying beside him, covered in blood. Everything else was the same as usual, which seemed—wrong, somehow.'

I knew what she meant; it must have seemed shocking that everything in the room was not defiled by the grotesque happening.

'And you phoned the police.'

'Yes, sir.'

'And they rounded up everyone in the building and as many as they could trace who'd been at the party?'

'That's right.'

So there it was. I relaxed a little.

'Well, Miss Barton? Any ideas?'

'Were there no finger prints?' I asked, remembering television serials.

'Nothing suspicious; the ornament had been wiped, but that was all. They reckon he must have opened the door using a handkerchief and not touched anything else.'

'Another cup of tea, sir?'

'No, thank you, Mrs Statton, we've taken up enough of your time. Thank you for being so patient with us.'

Matthew rose and so did I. It was only just after four, but the bleak day was already drawing in. Mrs Statton brought our macs, which had not had a chance to dry. A drop of rain fell from them on to the cat, which rippled its fur in protest. I turned away as Matthew pressed a note into Mrs Statton's hand, then we were running down to the car again, battered by the rain.

'A pretty fruitless journey, I'm afraid,' Matthew remarked. 'We'll just have a look at the apartment building while we're there, for you to get the idea of the layout.'

The idea of visiting the scene of crime did not appeal to me, especially on such a dismal afternoon, but I made no comment and after a few minutes' driving Matthew stopped and again we ran through the rain to the shelter of a doorway. But this was very different from Mrs Statton's humble little house.

Swing doors led us precipitately into an enormous marble-floored hall, against the far wall of which stood two pairs of lifts. On our immediate right was an alcove, barred by a counter with telephone and pigeon holes. From behind it, the hall porter was eyeing us questioning. He was tall and ruddy-faced, with a toothbrush moustache and carried himself well in his uniform.

An ex-soldier, I thought.

'Good afternoon sir, madam. Can I help you?' Then his eyes took in Matthew. 'Oh—it's you, sir. Mr—Haig, wasn't it?'

'Well done, Dawson. Yes, Matthew Haig. This is my secretary, Miss Barton. I wonder if we could have one more look along the corridor upstairs?'

'Well, sir, if I was to accompany you I don't see that it would matter.'

We moved over to the lifts. 'Self-operated, you see,' Matthew said to me, 'so no convenient liftman with a good memory.'

'I'm sure Mr Dawson is as good as any liftman,' I said tactfully, and was rewarded with an appreciative smile from behind the bristling moustache.

'Well, miss'—as a mere secretary I was no longer addressed as madam—'I always say, once I see a face, I remember it. And can usually put a name to it, too.'

The lift stopped and we got out on the second floor. A long, deeply-carpeted corridor swept in both directions, an arrow pointing to numbers 21 to 25 to our left, 26 to 30 to our right.

'Number 23 it was,' remarked Dawson. 'Can't let you in, I'm afraid—there's a new owner there now.'

We moved down the passage and stopped outside a royal blue door. The gilt number 23 gleamed on the paintwork and a card read, 'Fredericks, Major P.C.'

I thought suddenly, I'm standing where the murderer stood! and a frisson lifted my hair.

'And the party was just opposite,' Matthew said, looking at the door facing us, with its matching gilt number.

'That's right, sir. Young Mr Gilman. His parents were away on a cruise and he seized the opportunity, as you might say.'

'I suppose you didn't know the guests?'

'That I did not, sir, nor wouldn't want to, neither. A very strange bunch, to my way of thinking. Not a decent haircut among them.'

'How old is Mr Gilman?' I asked suddenly, and Matthew glanced at me in surprise.

Dawson ran his fingers through his moustache. 'Twenty-three, twenty-four.'

'So his guests were about that age too?'

'Anything from seventeen to thirty, I'd say.'

'In which case,' I mused, 'the murderer must also be a young man—or woman.'

Matthew turned questioningly, and Dawson nodded approval.

'Well,' I explained, 'the only reason he or she wasn't spotted was because a lot of other *young* people were in the building that night. A stranger who didn't fit in that age group would, I'm sure, be remembered by Mr Dawson.'

'My God,' Matthew said slowly. 'No doubt the police have registered that, but I confess it hadn't struck me. Well done, Emily.'

'Which,' I finished with a smile, 'disposes of several fictitious characters at least.'

'I suppose you know all the members of Mr Menzies' family, Dawson?'

'Oh yes, sir. Miss Lesley-that-was, and Mr Holloway, and Mr Jack Menzies and his wife—'

'And they weren't here that night?'

'Certainly not!' Dawson looked shocked, as well he might, considering the implications behind Matthew's question.

'And there's no one, Dawson, no one at all, who made an impression, who arrived by himself, perhaps, or didn't seem to fit in with the others?'

'No sir, I can't say there was.'

I said suddenly, 'You'd have noticed, wouldn't you, if someone had come down again almost straight away?'

'Yes, miss. But they reckon he ran down the service stairs and out the basement door.'

'He couldn't have come in that way, and avoided being seen at all?' Matthew asked hopefully, mindful of his plot.

'No, sir. The door was locked on the inside. The murderer unlocked it to let hisself out.'

'No doubt wiping the handle and key when he'd done so,' said Matthew resignedly.

'Quite so, sir.'

Money again changed hands and Matthew and I were back in the car. I gave a little shiver.

'Cold?' he asked. 'Or is it just distaste for the job?'

'A bit of both, suppose.'

'Well, let's go and have a drink somewhere, followed by a decent meal. That'll make you feel better.'

We drove to a hotel whose neon lights struck a note of cheer in the near-darkness. Matthew parked the car. 'Now, leave your notebooks. We've done enough work for one day.'

He took my arm and led me across the gleaming wet car-park, up the steps and through more swing doors. 'If you'd like to leave your mac in the cloakroom, I'll meet you back here.'

Gratefully, I escaped and did my best to right the havoc the wet afternoon had done to my hair. When I returned, Matthew rose from a table near the fire.

'What would you like to drink? Gin? Sherry?'

'Sherry, please.' He pulled out my chair and I sat down. We were early and there were not many people about. My mind was still on the interviews we'd had that afternoon.

'Mr Haig—'

Matthew set down his glass. 'I think while we're on a social footing we might dispense with formality, don't you?'

'Oh—yes, of course,' I stammered.

'Well? What were you going to say?'

'I was wondering how closely you intend sticking to the facts. I know neither the victim nor any of the other characters are like those in real life, but the setting is similar—the apartment block and the party.'

'Which is why I wanted another look.'

'Yes, but what I'm trying to say is that, in fiction as well as fact, the age of the party guests limits the choice of murderer.'

'Choice of murderer!' He laughed. 'What a

glorious phrase! I suppose it does, yes, but let's forget about it for now. If we never speak of anything else, it'll go stale on us. Agreed? No shop talk.'

'No shop!' I replied.

He raised his glass to me with a smile, and I realized with a sense of shock that it was the first he'd ever given me; very different from the sardonic twists I was used to. The effect was disconcerting; he seemed at once younger and more attractive. If he exercised this charm on Kate, I didn't see how she could resist him.

I relaxed in turn, and for the first time found I could be completely natural with him. Also for the first time, we were giving each other our undivided attention, as though no one else was in the room. But there were others present, of course—other women in particular, who, I noticed from quick glances, were very much aware of Matthew, and the knowledge made my self-confidence soar. We laughed a lot; I hadn't enjoyed myself so much for a long time. The evenings with Mike were never undiluted pleasure.

And hard on that thought came the realisation that I was bracketing Matthew and Mike together—which was dangerous. For Matthew was not a carefree young man with whom it was natural to flirt. He was one of Britain's best-known contemporary writers, a bitter, divorced man—with a daughter.

I laid my fork on my plate, and the little

tinkle put a full stop to my laughter.

'Had enough? Room for coffee and liqueur?'

'I'd love a coffee, thank you, but nothing else.'

'What a modest little mouse you are! Go on, try one!'

I did not like being called a mouse, modest or otherwise. 'All right.'

The unaccustomed drink brought back my confidence and made me more than a little heady. Matthew lit a cigar and the pungent smoke cocooned us in our small world of candles and coffee cups. I wished that we could drift for ever shut off from all uncomfortable influences. No Mike, no Derek, no Kate.

But Matthew was already looking at his watch. 'Well, since it's a two-hour drive home in the dark, we'd better be going. Would you like to collect your mac while I get the bill?'

In the cloakroom mirror I caught sight of my face, unusually flushed and bright-eyed. Not, I thought tartly, the face of a secretary who has just been given dinner by her boss. Hastily I shrugged on my mac and went out into the hall. Matthew was waiting by the door. The rain had lessened and was now a misty drizzle. He took my arm and guided me over to the car, and we eased our way out of the car park into the still-busy streets of the town. It was only about nine o'clock, but the wet darkness made it seem later. Matthew switched on the radio and my eyes, smarting still from the cigar smoke and the sweet potency of the liqueur, closed. I leant back, half-listening to the quiet music, aware of the turning and swaying of the car. Against my eyelids swam jumbled pictures of the day's events—work that morning in the library, the drive out—Mrs Statton—Dawson in the thick-carpeted passage—Matthew's smile above the candles.

I think I slept for a while. I was jerked awake by the car swerving, and heard Matthew swear under his breath. I pushed myself upright.

'Sorry. A dog ran across the road.'

Moorland now stretched on either side of us and the headlights carved a gleaming path over the wet road. In their beam the rain fell glancingly. The wipers burred rhythmically, almost in time to the soft music on the radio. They reminded me of the metronome during music lessons at school.

The thought of school brought Sarah to mind. She would be home tomorrow, Saturday. I'd promised to play with her. If only Matthew would spend some time with her. I glanced at him. He was softly whistling the tune on the radio, his eyes on the road. The air of companionship was still between us. I began tentatively, 'I suppose it's none of my business—'

He smiled. 'Then whatever it is, forget it!'

I should have taken his advice. Instead, foolishly counting on the evening behind us to give me immunity, I went on, 'It's about Sarah—'

'What about Sarah?' He spoke pleasantly, but the danger signal was there. I chose to ignore it. I should have remembered his reaction to my speaking of boarding school on the outward journey. I should have remembered any number of things, and kept quiet.

But I didn't. 'I wish you were nicer to her!' I blurted out.

I felt rather than saw his eyebrows rise. 'Aren't you presuming rather, Miss Barton?'

Even the resurrection of 'Miss Barton' couldn't stop me now. This had been on my mind so much that once I embarked on the subject I was powerless to stop. 'I'm sorry if you're annoyed, but she tries so hard to get a bit of your attention. Yet if you notice her at all, it's only to say, "Go to bed, Sarah." Or, "Haven't you any homework?" or, "I'm busy." ' I paused for breath.

'Quite a speech.' There was a dangerous note in his voice, but I plunged recklessly ahead.

'She showed me her photograph album, and there's not a single snap of the three of you as a family—not one. Because she was never with you! First her mother deserts her, then you—'

'That will do!' Matthew's voice was a whiplash. I had gone too far.

Panic-stricken, I belatedly tried to withdraw, to gloss over. 'She once—'

'I said *that will do*!' The car suddenly swerved into a lay-by and shuddered to a halt. Matthew turned towards me. His face was in shadow but I could see the tightness of his jaw, and I knew he was very angry.

'Now, Miss Emily Barton,' he said with biting deliberation, 'let's get one thing straight. I engaged you as my secretary, not as a child-welfare officer. I will take no advice on bringing up my daughter from a tinpot little typist. Is that clear?'

I could only stare at him while the vicious words lashed the air between us.

'*Is that clear*?'

'Yes,' I whispered aridly.

'Good.' Without warning his arm snaked along the back of the seat towards me and pulled me roughly against him. I fell with a little gasp and as I did so, his mouth came down on mine, bruisingly and ruthlessly. I clung to him more to keep my balance than for any other reason.

After a moment he pushed me unceremoniously away, turned round again and switched on the ignition. 'Now will you shut up?' he said shakily, and the car leapt ahead into the night.

I sat immobile, my face burning and the rest

of my body like ice. So the party was over. I had expended my ration of his charm. I was a tinpot little typist who had presumed upon his relaxation to butt in where she was not wanted. Right, Mr Matthew Haig, that's the last time I'll presume, I promise you!

Once or twice, I felt Matthew glance at me, but we did not speak again during the whole, interminable journey home. He was driving extremely fast. Trees and houses rushed towards us along the beam of our headlights, towered over us like monstrous shadows, and were gone, swinging crazily as we slewed round corners with a scream of rubber on wet tarmac. I didn't care. If Matthew was in such a hurry to get this evening over, that went for me too.

It was, of course, my own fault, I assured myself. Who did I think I was, to criticize Matthew Haig? A few drinks and smiles in the candlelight did not entitle me to speak to my employer as I had done.

I did not let myself think about the kiss.

I had my front door key ready when we finally hurtled up the road and through the gates of Touchstone. He still had his foot on the brake as I wrenched open the car door and ran up the steps into the house.

CHAPTER NINE

When I had eaten as much as I could face of my breakfast the next morning, I took a moment or two to screw up my courage before going down to Matthew. I'd spent most of the night lying staring into the dark till my eyes burned, trying to think of the right thing to say to him. It was partly his fault I told myself; if he'd not been so charming and attentive all evening, I should never have dared speak to him as I did—and even then, it was only my fondness for Sarah that had compelled me to put in a word for her. Though what had possessed me to mention Kate—I went hot at the memory.

As for the kiss, it had been simply a working off of his bad temper; since he could hardly have hit me, he'd used an alternative means of bringing me to order. Through the closed door I heard the hall clock strike nine. The time for decisions had run out; I'd have to take my cue from him. With hammering heart I went down to the library.

It was at once apparent that my heart-searching had been needless. Whatever his mood last night, this morning Matthew Haig was fully in control of himself and the situation. He was sitting at his desk as usual, reading some papers.

I said, 'Good morning, Mr Haig,' and marvelled at the steadiness of my voice.

'Good morning. Would you type out yesterday's notes first, please?'

'Of course.' I seated myself at my desk, and took the cover off my typewriter with shaking fingers. He had not raised his head. I shot a furtive glance at the intent face, black brows drawn together in concentration, and tried to equate it with the charming companion of the previous evening. Then I closed my mind to the comparison and settled down to work.

After a while I rose and put the completed pages on his desk.

'Thank you. Have you got your book?' He looked up and my own eyes automatically dropped.

'Yes.'

'Well, it looks as though, after what we discovered yesterday, we'll have to do a spot of rewriting. The daughter and the brother episodes will have to be altered. Obviously the doorman would have known them both.'

I spoke before I remembered my resolution to volunteer nothing. 'Does there have to be a doorman in the novel?'

He gave a short laugh. 'Admittedly it would be easier without him.' He paused, stroking his chin. 'The point is, though, that I'd wanted to work as much as possible within the framework of the case, to see if I could pinpoint the motive. I like to think I'm as intelligent as the average murderer.'

I did not rise to that one but waited silently, my eyes on my book. He seemed to be expecting some comment, and I realized that we'd developed the habit of discussing problems which arose in the plot. Well, not any more. Tinpot typists don't have any ideas of their own.

I sat smarting under my hurt pride, and after a moment he said, 'Well, leave the rewriting for now and I'll think about it when I've had time to study these notes. Where were we up to?'

I read back the last page I'd typed before we left for Salchester. He dictated steadily until it was almost twelve.

'That will do for now.'

I stood up.

'Emily—' He made a movement with his hand to detain me, and I stiffened. But before either of us could speak, the sound of flying footsteps reached us from the passage, and the door burst open as Sarah fell into the room. Her face was flushed and her eyes bright with excitement.

'Daddy, Mummy's come! She's here now!'

Matthew rose slowly to his feet. His face went scarlet, then the colour ebbed away, leaving it very white.

A voice from the doorway said, 'Well, darling, where's the red carpet?'

I was too numbed by the suddenness of

events to do anything but stare at the woman who stood there. She was tall and thin—almost angular—and dressed very correctly in the Londoner's idea of 'country clothes'. Her face was oval, framed by short, curly chestnut hair, and her deep set eyes were a penetrating blue.

I heard Matthew say, 'Kate!'

She gave a light laugh. 'The very same!'

'Kate,' he said again, coming round from behind his desk. He went over to her, took both her hands and kissed her cheek.

'That's a little better! And this is your new secretary, is it? How do you do?' She disengaged one of her hands from Matthew's and held it out to me.

I moved forward and took it. 'How do you do, Mrs . . .' I floundered helplessly.

'The name is still Haig—for the moment.'

Matthew cleared his throat. 'Kate, it's wonderful to see you. Forgive me, it was such a surprise! How long can you stay?'

'You mean when am I going back? No, don't deny it! As it happens, I'm not in any particular rush—say three or four days, if you'll have me. I felt it was time I saw my daughter again.' Her arm went casually round Sarah's neck, and the child's face glowed with pleasure. Well, now I had my family group, the three of them momentarily framed in the doorway.

A voice called, 'Miss Kate? Is that you?' and Miss Tamworth came hurrying down the passage.

'Hello, Tammy!' Kate stooped and kissed the withered cheek. 'Have you been rearing my chick properly? She looks a credit to you!' And she smiled at Sarah again with careless affection.

I felt horribly in the way, but Matthew relieved me. 'Come to the sitting-room and have a drink. Tammy'll take your cases up. Have you come straight from London? You must be exhausted.'

They moved, the three of them, still in a close circle, out of the room. I could hear them talking and Kate's laugh as they went up the hall. Only when I heard the sitting-room door close did I draw breath. Now the household was complete; the family was in the sitting-room, the secretary in the library. A nice distinction. I returned to my desk and began to type.

Mrs Johnson came to tell me when lunch was ready. I was surprised to see her, since she'd left after breakfast as usual, to spend the weekend with her daughter.

'The mistress collected me on her way through,' she told me beamingly, not at all put out by having her weekend disrupted. 'Doesn't want to spend her time cooking and cleaning on her visit, now does she? Ah, 'tis lovely to see her again. You mark my words, dearie, one of these days she'll be back for good. The master's a different man when she's here!'

Sourly I followed her down the passage. As we reached the main hall the telephone started to ring and Kate, who was coming out of the sitting-room with Matthew, lifted it. 'Hello? No, this is Mrs Haig. Mike? Oh darling, how lovely!'

I stopped awkwardly, knowing the call was for me.

'Yes, I've just arrived . . . I'm not sure; it depends. Look, sweetie, when can we see you? Tonight? What—Emily? Is that her name? How quaint! Yes, she's here. I'll pass you over then. Bye, darling.'

She held out the instrument to me. 'Let's drop the formality, shall we? You're Emily, I'm Kate.'

It was impossible to resist the brilliance of her smile. 'Persuade Mike to come round this evening, there's an angel; I haven't seen him for ages. Is he still as handsome?'

Without waiting for my confused reply to this torrent, she linked her arm through Matthew's and went with him into the dining-room.

'Hello, Mike.' How flat my voice must have sounded after Kate's.

'Hi there. Sorry I haven't been in touch. One of the cows has just calved and we had a difficult time with her. In fact, I spent two nights in the byre. Fine little bull calf, though.'

Not a word about our last encounter. Perhaps sufficient time had elapsed for it to be ignored.

'I was going to suggest we hit some high spot tonight, but Kate's invited me round there. Is that all right with you?'

An evening sharing Mike with Kate and Matthew! How different from last night, when there had just been Matthew and me. I said hurriedly, 'Yes, of course, that's fine.'

'What do you think of Kate? Isn't she fabulous?'

'Fabulous,' I echoed drily.

'See you tonight then, about eight. ' 'Bye, angel.'

Thoughtfully, I replaced the receiver.

* * *

It wasn't until later that it occurred to me I wasn't the only one who might find the evening awkward. Matthew would surely rather have had Kate to himself her first evening. Things between Mike and himself were strained, and his only social contact with me had not been an unqualified success.

'Come to the sitting-room when you're ready, Emily,' Kate said, quite naturally taking her place as mistress of the house. 'As you'll have gathered, I've persuaded Mrs Johnson to stay this weekend. I couldn't have faced spending the evening in the kitchen!'

And Mrs Johnson, dear soul, was under the impression that she was helping bring Kate and Matthew together again. As well she might be.

'Oh, and would you ask her to light the fire in the library passage? It's much cosier than being alone in the sitting-room when you and Matthew are working. It was always my special place, wasn't it, darling?'

So the fire was lit and remained so for the rest of Kate's stay. I was surprised at the transformation it made to the end of the passage. Kate even drew the miniature velvet curtains over the oriel windows, creating an air of warmth and friendliness in what had been merely a utilitarian passageway.

That first evening, Kate changed into a silk blouse of pale coffee and an ankle-length skirt in a deeper brown. The length of her skirt, from which her ankles emerged as bony and fragile as those of a racehorse, added to her height and slimness, and her long white neck rose gracefully from the low-necked blouse. I thought a little uncharitably that her shoulders were too thin for such a neckline—her collar-bones were almost as prominent above the clinging silk of her blouse as were her small breasts beneath it. The total effect, however, was one of gracious elegance and made me feel about twelve years old.

She held the stage that night, talking lightly and incessantly, mainly to Mike—about the plays she'd seen, the books she'd read, the articles she planned. The pattern was set before dinner, and continued both during the meal and afterwards, over coffee in the sitting-room.

Matthew and I sat throughout in comparative silence, while I watched him and he watched Kate. He hardly seemed able to drag his eyes away from her, but I couldn't read the expression in them.

And it was over coffee that I felt the first stirrings of anxiety, an awareness that all was not well. It seemed that things were spinning out of control, as though we were on some brightly-lit stage, speaking words that had been written for us and could not be changed. This, I thought fancifully, was the opening scene, introducing the characters before the play got under way and the tragedy began. Tragedy? Startled, I wondered what had brought that word so naturally to mind.

I studied the three faces more carefully. How, as a theatre director, would I gauge them? First Kate, relaxed in her chair with a glass in her hand. The firelight struck sparks in the amber depths of her hair, as I'd seen it do in her daughter's. Her laugh was brittle and gay. Was she really as much on the surface as she tried to appear, or was there something deep down that troubled her? And was it my imagination that her eyes grew wary when they flicked in Matthew's direction?

And Matthew himself; as I turned to him my uneasiness increased. The lamp behind him threw his face into shadow, but his eyes, dark and unlit, remained on his ex-wife. What was going through his mind?

Mike was also watching Kate, a smile on his face. He looked so much the same as usual, with one leg carelessly crossed high over the other, that I longed to slip over to him and take his hand.

Yet even as the thought formed, his attention suddenly focussed. Something came and went so swiftly behind his eyes that had I not been watching them in that instant, I should have missed it. I moved sharply, wondering whether the coldness in me came from a draught, or from something more sinister.

'Found out something?' he was repeating, and his voice was idly curious, a world away from the flicker I thought I'd seen. 'My dear Kate, how mysterious! Tell us more!'

'I'm not sure that I shall.' Her eyes rested on Matthew, and there was a malicious gleam in them that I certainly wasn't imagining. 'But perhaps I should admit, my love, that it wasn't only an irresistible longing to see you that brought me hotfoot to Cornwall.'

Matthew stirred. The firelight leapt across his face and receded. 'What, then?'

'Work; we're doing a series on old country houses in the West Country, Touchstone among them. I was asked to come down and vet them all, but first, for background, I needed to know how long they'd been in the same family, who'd been born where, and so on. So—' Her eyes moved lazily from one of us to another—'I went to St Catherine's House, where, I might say, I spent a most informative morning.'

'St Catherine's House?' Matthew repeated sharply.

'Yes; I'd no idea what a treasure-trove it would prove. I discovered all kinds of family secrets.'

There was a taut silence, and I found I was holding my breath.

Then Matthew said, 'An ancestor was hanged for sheep-stealing?'

'Rather more recent than that.' She sipped at her drink, no longer looking at him.

'Exactly what are you getting at, Kate?'

She shrugged. 'I thought I should warn you, before it comes out in print.'

'You really intend to dig up some long-forgotten gossip and *publish* it?'

'Why not? It's a good story. A very good story.'

Mike said lightly, 'Do we assume, Mrs Haig, that the family honour means nothing to you?'

'Less than nothing, darling.'

Matthew leant forward and threw his cigarette in the fire. 'Is this an attempt at blackmail, by any chance?'

I gasped, but Kate merely raised her eyebrows.

'Because if so,' he went on, 'you'll be disappointed. Who do you imagine would be remotely interested in your sordid little findings?'

'A lot of people,' Kate answered, sipping her drink, 'believe me. However, the question of blackmail, as you so charmingly term it, doesn't arise, since I've no intention of being bought off. Really, Matthew—' her voice was mocking—'you're rising to my bait even better than I'd hoped.'

The menace in the room was tangible.

Matthew said under his breath, 'God damn you, Kate.'

Mike moved uneasily. 'Come on, Kate, this has gone far enough. Did you really discover something?'

'I did.'

'Then take my advice and forget it.' He glanced at Matthew. 'Or you might really stir up a hornets' nest. Your paper won't thank you if you land them in the libel courts.'

Kate's eyes swivelled to me. 'What must Emily think of us all? Such bad form to wash the family linen in public.'

'So far,' Matthew said with a certain acid humour, 'you've not even opened the laundry basket.'

Kate laughed. 'Right—a truce! What shall we talk about now?'

Mike looked up as the clock on the mantelpiece chimed eleven.

'As far as I'm concerned, it's time for bed,' he said. 'I have to be up at five.'

'Is there such a time?' Kate hid a delicate yawn behind her hand. 'We'll see you tomorrow, though, won't we? You can spare some time later to visit your long-lost cousin, or whatever?'

Mike grinned, reached down and pulled her to her feet. 'Kate, to see you I would move mountains!' He kissed her on the mouth.

Matthew said shortly, 'I'll see you out, then.'

Kate turned. 'Don't be so obtuse, Matthew—let Emily! I've monopolised Mike all evening, and it was supposed to be her date. Let them at least say goodnight in private.'

Matthew said stiffly, 'Of course.'

I felt unwelcome colour flood my face. But Mike, unabashed, winked at me and reached for my hand. 'Well, goodnight—thanks for the meal. Anyone going down to the beach tomorrow?' His eyes included me.

I shook my head. 'I don't think so.'

'Oh, I shall,' Kate said. 'I'm not going to waste a chance to sunbathe!'

Mike hesitated, and I realized his difficulty. 'Well, we'll see how it goes. Thanks again.'

We left the room hand in hand and he closed the door behind us. The large hall was in darkness except for the huge shadows on the ceiling from the fire round the corner. Without preamble he drew me into his arms. I wished Kate hadn't made the kiss so inevitable. I didn't really feel like kissing Mike tonight. I moved a little and his lips went to my hair.

'That was one hell of an evening.'

'Yes.'

'Oh Emily, it's been a long week.'

'Only four days, actually.'

'Only?'

'A very long four days,' I amended. Made even longer by what had happened in the interim. Could Matthew kiss as tenderly as this? I wondered involuntarily, and my heart jerked like an exposed nerve.

Mike raised his head. 'What is it?'

'Nothing, nothing!' Gently I extricated myself.

'Goodnight, Mike,' I said, with an unsteady smile.

'Goodnight, sweetheart. See you tomorrow.' He lifted my fingers to his lips and kissed them gently. Then he opened the front door and was gone.

I paused uncertainly outside the sitting-room door. There was complete silence inside. With clenched fists stiffly at my side, I marched up the stairs to bed.

CHAPTER TEN

I had my breakfast upstairs the next morning, despite its being Sunday, since Mrs Johnson was with us. When she brought my tray, she passed on the message that Matthew would be in the library at ten o'clock.

Business as usual, I thought grimly. In the clear light of day, my morbid imaginings of the night before seemed ludicrous and I dismissed them from my mind.

The fire was already burning in the hall, although the day was milder and the sun breaking through the massed clouds. It made the passage oppressively warm. I found that Matthew, no doubt of the same mind, had flung open the French windows in the library and was standing gazing out over the lawn.

He acknowledged my arrival merely with a gesture of his hand. After sitting in silence for a while, I said tentatively, 'Shall I read back what we did yesterday?'

'Um?'

'Would you—?'

'Oh—yes.' He turned from the window, and I noticed dark rims under his eyes. It seemed he'd slept no better than I had. 'Yes, please.'

Usually a few minutes of this was enough to restart his train of thought, but today he didn't stop me, letting me read the entire passage.

When I stopped there was another silence.

He moved back to his desk, sat down and rubbed his hands over his face. 'I don't seem to be thinking very clearly this morning. I'm sorry, I'm wasting your time.'

'It's all right,' I murmured awkwardly.

'Are you seeing Mike today?'

I looked up in surprise. 'I think we all are, aren't we? Kate—I mean Mrs Haig—'

'Oh yes, of course. He didn't—?' he broke off.

'Didn't what?'

'Nothing. Oh hell, look I really am sorry. My brain just isn't functioning today.'

'Shall I make you some coffee? That might clear your head.'

'Would you? I'd be very grateful.'

I put my blank notebook on the chair and opened the library door. And there was Kate, comfortably ensconced in one of the leather armchairs with the Sunday papers. She was wearing royal blue trousers and a cherry-red top. She looked, I thought acidly, as though she were on the deck of a luxury liner.

'That was a brief session,' she remarked.

'We haven't started yet. I'm going to make some coffee.'

'Be an angel and bring me a cup, too.'

I nodded and walked stiffly down the passage, aware of her eyes following me. In the kitchen, Mrs Johnson turned in surprise from peeling potatoes.

'We'd like our coffee a little early this morning,' I told her. 'It's all right, you carry on—I'll do it.'

'Very well, miss. Thank you. Is Madam down yet?'

I bit my lip. 'Yes, I'm making a cup for her, too.'

'The fire's going all right, is it?'

'It's fine.'

The percolator seemed to take for ever. I stood watching it, holding my mind carefully blank. When at last it was ready, I poured the coffee into three cups and added milk, watching the liquid change into the colour of Kate's blouse the night before.

'Would you like some, Mrs Johnson? There's plenty.'

'No thank you, my dear. Can't say as I fancy it. I'll make myself a nice pot of tea when I've finished they potatoes.'

She put the cups on a cloth-covered tray, and opened the door for me. I carried it carefully down the passage.

Kate uncurled herself like a cat and reached for her cup. 'If you're not working, have yours here with me.'

I hesitated. 'I think we'll be starting as soon as we've had this.'

She smiled, and the tiny electric current pricked again at my spine. 'Ask him.'

I opened the library door. Matthew was sitting as I'd left him, his head resting in his hands.

'Mrs Haig is out here—will you join her for coffee?'

He looked up. 'Very well.' He came out of the room with my desk chair in his hand. 'No, it's all right, Miss Barton, you sit there—I'll have this one.'

' "Miss Barton"!' Kate mimicked, as I seated myself in the second armchair. 'God, you're so stuffy, Matthew! Call the child Emily, and be done with it!'

Matthew's face whitened.

I said quickly, 'This is in working hours, Kate.'

'And he's always pompous when you're working? How do you put up with it?'

As I struggled to find a reply, Matthew commented, 'Since I so obviously annoy you, I'm surprised you asked me to join you.'

She turned on him a smile of false sweetness. 'Actually, I didn't. I invited Emily, and she asked you.'

'I see. Then I beg your pardon.'

'Oh, stop it, both of you!' I broke in before I could prevent myself. Matthew's head jerked in my direction, and Kate raised her delicate eyebrows.

'I'm—sorry,' I muttered.

'Not at all—Emily—it's we who should apologize.' Matthew drained his cup and replaced it on the tray. 'Thanks for the coffee, but I'm afraid it hasn't worked. I'm still not in the mood for work, so I'll go straight down to the golf club. The rest of the day is your own.'

'Will you be back for lunch?' Kate asked.

'Probably not, I'll eat there.' He stood up, carried the chair back into the library, and came out again, closing the door behind him. He looked down at us and I thought for a moment he was going to say something. Then he apparently changed his mind and disappeared down the passage.

Kate laughed.

I said involuntarily, 'Why do you try to hurt him all the time?'

'Oh I don't,' she said softly, 'Not *all* the time.'

I stood up. 'I'm afraid it's rather warm for me here. I think I'll take Sarah for a walk—she'll be at Sunday school this afternoon.' I'd forgotten I was speaking to the child's mother till I saw her amused smile. I wondered whether to apologize, ask permission or include her in the invitation, but before I could make up my mind she reached down for the newspaper and I made my escape.

It was a blue and gold day, with autumn in the air. Sarah, delighted at the unexpected outing, skipped and danced at my side.

'Let's go to the farm and see Uncle Mike!' she suggested.

'He'll probably be busy, though he did say there was a new calf.'

We had already turned up the track. The

high spiky hedges were jewelled with berries and the gorse at our feet was yellowing. A heavy dew still lay on the thick grass where the sun had not reached. Above us the sky was clear and an aeroplane, droning like a sleepy bee, left a cobweb of white across the blue.

Sarah said suddenly, 'I told you Mummy was beautiful, didn't I?'

In the eye of the beholder, no doubt, I thought, smiling down at her. 'You did.' I confirmed. But was she? She was finely drawn, a thoroughbred, with her long neck, her lean body and slender feet. She was vibrant and tantalising; she was elegant and carelessly sophisticated, but her nose was too thin and her eyes too deep-set for beauty, and her warm, passionate mouth belonged in a softer face. As hard as nails, I thought, and was surprised by my vehemence.

But Sarah was satisfied and ran on ahead of me, startling some sheep which bucked clumsily out of the way like frightened hearth rugs. Now that we were climbing, the sea became visible again, still and blue in the bay.

'I wish I didn't have Sunday school,' Sarah said rebelliously. 'Mummy said she's going to the beach this afternoon.'

'Perhaps she'll still be there when you get back.'

Sarah pouted. 'And I'll be at school all day tomorrow. I don't seem to have seen her at all!'

'You were with her yesterday,' I reminded her.

Sarah nodded.

'Do you know what? She asked if I'd like to live in London!'

I stopped, frowning. 'And would you?'

She clasped her hands. 'Oh, yes! Seeing the Queen, and Big Ben, and everything!'

I laughed. 'You wouldn't see much of the Queen, poppet!'

'But she lives in London, doesn't she?'

It was impossible to explain the vastness of the city to this country child, whose world was bounded by the comfortable friendliness of Chapelcombe. 'London's a big place,' I said lamely.

Sarah's dragonfly mind darted on to something else, but I wondered for a while what had prompted Kate to ask the question.

Chapel Farm lay gleaming in the sunshine. As we approached, a man in corduroy trousers came out of the stables and stopped on seeing us. Then he smiled shyly at me and said, 'Your uncle baint here, Miss Sarah. Had to go out early this morning.'

'Benson, can we see the new calf?'

'Ah, so it's the little fella you're interested in! Right-ho then, come along.'

He touched his forehead to me in a delightfully old-world gesture and led the way into the clean, pungently sweet-smelling byre. It was warm, and sunlight filtered through the door on to the clean straw which lay on the floor. Benson went ahead of us and slapped gently at the brown and cream hindquarters of the animal in the end stall. 'Move over, lass, and let Miss Sarah see the little un.'

'Oh!' Sarah gasped ecstatically. The tiny animal stood beside its mother, great mournful eyes staring up at us, and twitching tail. 'What's he called?'

'Well now, he's entered in the book as Stacey's Pride, but I own we don't call un that!'

Sarah's eyes were still fixed on the enchanting little creature. 'What do you call him, then?'

Benson laughed and scratched his head. 'Up to now I been calling un Titch!'

'Titch', Sarah repeated. 'That's what Uncle Mike used to call me, but I'm too big now.'

Across her head the cowman's kindly eyes met mine. Sarah reached out a hand to scratch the top of the head between the silken bumps that would grow into horns. The little animal lifted his head back and rolled his long, rough tongue round her fingers.

'No milk there,' smiled Benson and Sarah gasped as the searching tongue rasped her flesh. The cow turned her head and watched us with liquid eyes, but she appeared to accept our admiration with equanimity. The delicate ears flicked back and forth.

'We must be going, Sarah,' I said quietly, 'or we'll be late for lunch.' I turned to Benson.

'Thank you for letting us look at him.'

We walked out of the dim stall into the bright sunlight of the cobbled yard.

'I wish I lived on a farm!' Sarah exclaimed, relinquishing the Queen without a backward glance.

I smiled and took her hand. 'Come along, I'll race you to the top of the hill!'

Matthew kept to his intention of lunching at the golf club and the rest of us had a light-hearted meal. Sarah chatted incessantly about the calf and how she wished she lived on a farm. I saw Kate's eyes on her speculatively, but she made no comment.

The bracing walk had cleared my head of any lingering uneasiness and I was ready to shrug off my nebulous fears as heightened imagination. Impossible to suppose there could be any threat to us, sitting here in the sun-filled dining-room.

'Do change your mind and come down to the beach Emily!' Kate urged me.

'Well . . .' I wasn't too anxious for her company.

'Please!' she added.

'All right. I suppose after the end of the month there won't be many more chances to go.'

'You are lucky—' Sarah began.

'Hush, Sarah,' interposed Miss Tamworth. 'You've had a long summer holiday, but Sunday afternoons are set aside for church, as well you know.'

'Mummy doesn't go to church,' Sarah protested.

'That,' said Miss Tamworth with a glint in her eye, 'is her affair.' I had myself seen Miss Tamworth setting off in unbecoming grey as I made my way to the library that morning.

'Mummy is beyond redemption,' said Kate lightly, and again I felt the extra-sensory quiver.

Miss Tamworth frowned reprovingly and Sarah said with her mouth full, 'What's redemption?'

'Nothing you need trouble your head about,' retorted Miss Tamworth sharply.

Kate tossed her napkin on the table and stood up. 'See you at tea, Sarah. Put in a prayer for me! Come on, Emily.'

Silently I followed her from the room and we went upstairs to collect our beach things. We did not speak as we walked together down the path to the main road. There was an offshore breeze and as we came out of the shelter of the high hedges it blew us forward with gusty breaths.

'I hope it will be warm enough down there,' I said doubtfully, remembering the blowing sand on my last visit.

'It will if we sit against the cliff. This is the bay where the girl was drowned, isn't it? Strange business, that.'

'Strange?'

'That she could have drowned on such a calm day. Apparently there wasn't a breath of wind.'

'I suppose if you can't swim, you can't swim, and that's all there is to it.'

'Perhaps you're right.' Kate slung a sweater over her shoulder and one of its sleeves knocked the sunglasses out of my hand. They landed on the grass just where the little track I'd noticed before ran round the face of the cliff.

'Do you know where that comes out?' I asked, as I bent to retrieve them.

'Not really—it probably meanders round to the next bay.' She waited for me to rejoin her, staring out to sea with her hand shading her eyes.

'I should keep to the inside edge,' I advised. 'It's very steep round the next corner.'

'Yes, I know.'

I flushed. Again, I'd forgotten that Kate wasn't a stranger here, and this wasn't the first time she'd been down to the bay. However, she didn't notice my confusion.

'What do you think of Mike?' she demanded.

I said evasively, 'He's good fun.'

'He's too good-looking by half,' Kate said shortly. 'It ensures that he always gets his own way.'

'Not with me, he won't!' I said emphatically, and she gave a brief laugh.

'Good for you!'

The sand was warm and soft sifting through my sandals. I was glad of the book I'd brought; I did not relish the thought of an entire afternoon's conversation with Kate.

We spread our rug up against the foot of the cliffs and she peeled off shirt and trousers. I huddled into mine, reluctant, for the moment, to undress. Kate's long legs seemed to go on for ever in her brief swimsuit. Her shadow, even longer legged, flickered up the cliff face behind us.

She sat down beside me and lit a cigarette. 'Don't you get bored to tears down here?' she asked, lifting her head and blowing a cloud of smoke into the air.

'I've only been here two weeks.'

'Two days is usually enough for me!'

'But you *were* here longer, surely? I mean—'

'When Matthew and I were together? I used to drag him up to London on the slightest pretext. He hated it. When I had to stay here, I invited friends down to liven things up. That caused more rows than anything.' She sat forward hugging her knees and gazing out to sea, her eyes narrowed against the cigarette smoke.

'I started spending the weeks in town and coming here only at weekends. It couldn't go on like that, and it didn't. That's all there was to it. I never dreamt Matthew meant to keep me down here all the time. It's not only that the place has been in the family so long—he actually seems to *like* it!'

I smiled in spite of myself. 'And that was two years ago?'

'Yes. Since then he's just had Sarah and Tammy for company, though I sometimes wondered about that blonde secretary of his.'

I moistened dry lips. 'Why?' The word was almost a croak.

Kate shrugged. 'No particular reason, except they were cooped up together all day.'

I said unwisely, 'Mike thinks he wants you back.'

She swung her head towards me with a look of almost idiotic surprise.

'*What*?'

I knew there was no need to repeat it, so I merely nodded confirmation. A slow smile broke over her face.

'Honestly? Well, that really is rich!'

There was a sudden, tinkling sound above us, and a tiny pebble landed on my lap. I looked up, and my whole body became an arch of terror. How I bunched my frozen muscles I don't know, but I leapt at Kate and knocked her sideways. Clutching hold of her, I rolled with her over the sand, the force of impact carrying us several yards, first one uppermost, then the other.

It seemed hours but could have been only thirty seconds from the pebble landing on my lap to the deafening crash that echoed through the rocks. I felt Kate's fingers dig convulsively into my shoulders.

There was a choking, blinding cloud of dust and sand. When it cleared, we saw that an enormous boulder, with dust already settling on it, lay squarely in the middle of our rug.

'God,' said Kate whitely, 'I think I'm going to be sick.'

'I'll be back in a minute!' Acting on blind impulse I jumped up and ran for the steps. I had not stopped to search for my sandals—they were probably under the boulder anyway—and the sharp flint knifed my feet. I hardly noticed it. Choking, gasping, legs on fire, I forced myself to run up the twisting, winding steps to the grass track, where I stopped, heart pounding, drawing in huge lungsful of air. There on the path, where I had dropped my sunglasses twenty minutes earlier, lay a ground-out cigarette. It had not been there before.

The fact reverberated round my head like crashing cymbals and the blood drummed sickeningly in my ears. My legs felt as though they might give way any minute, but I stepped carefully over the cigarette and started along the track, hardly knowing what I was doing, until, immediately below me, I could see the shattered boulder.

I inched forward. There was a depression in the grass where someone had been crouching. In the face of the cliff just below the track, exposed stone gaped rawly. The cavity where the boulder had lain was dank and rank-smelling. Little grey insects, suddenly exposed to the daylight, scurried obscenely in all directions.

It must have taken a very hard shove to dislodge it. I accepted the thought on a superficial level, refusing to examine it. Then a gull screamed discordantly, shattering my false calm, and I started to shake.

I must go back to Kate. For which of us had that gruesome death been planned?

I stumbled back the way I had come, head bent, eyes intent on the track, and cannoned into someone coming down the path. I heard myself scream and the sound went on ringing in my head.

Matthew's voice vibrated with shock. 'Emily, in God's name what is it?' His hands gripped me like iron clamps.

I couldn't answer him. I shook my head helplessly, seeming only to stand because he held me.

'Emily—speak to me! *What happened*?'

My tongue moved awkwardly in my dry mouth. At the second attempt the words came. 'A boulder—crashed down—on the rug—where we were sitting.' I couldn't look at his face.

'Kate?' The tone was urgent.

'She's all right.'

'Thank God!'

'Thank Emily would be more to the point!'

We both turned. Kate, ashen-faced and shivering in her emerald swimsuit, stood just below us on the path. 'If she hadn't pushed me clear, it would have been curtains for Kate Hardacre.'

'I can't believe it!' Matthew said. His eyes were like coals in his white face. He slipped off his jacket and draped it round Kate's bare shoulders. Then he took each of us by the arm, and we started back to the house.

Our return to Touchstone was nothing if not dramatic. Matthew flung open the front door and called, 'Tammy! Mrs Johnson! Rugs and hot-water bottles—quickly!'

I have a confused memory of their white, staring faces. Then Kate and I were firmly settled by the now-welcome fire in the passage, wrapped in rugs and sipping hot sweet tea.

Matthew moved about distractedly, staring from one of us to the other. After a while Kate stopped shuddering and raised her head from her cup to ask, 'Emily, why did you dash up the path like that?'

I'd been dreading the question. 'I—I thought I saw something.'

'And did you?' Matthew asked. His eyes were on me, dark, unfathomable, and waiting.

'No,' I said, then, since it seemed further explanation was needed, I added the first thing that came into my head. 'It must have been all the heavy rain that loosened it.'

There was a sudden crash as the front door swung open and banged against the wall.

'Emily? Emily, are you there?'

Matthew, his eyes on me, called, 'She's all right, Mike.'

'What in God's name happened?' Mike, as white as the rest of us, came quickly round the corner, stopping short as he saw Kate and me swathed in our rugs like a pair of old Indians.

'How did you know anything had?' Matthew asked, quietly.

Mike answered automatically. 'I came to look for them—here at the house first, because Emily said she wasn't going to the beach. There was no one in so I thought she must have changed her mind, and went home for my swimming gear. But when I got to the beach, there was a bloody great slab plum in the middle of the rug and Emily's sunglasses beside it. I thought—I didn't know what to think.'

Swiftly he came over, knelt in front of me and took my hands in his. I gripped them tightly. 'You really are all right, honey?'

'Yes, really Mike.' I could feel his heart hammering against my knees. He bent his head for a moment to my rug-swathed knees. There was a pulse beating in his temple and his forehead was sticky with sweat.

He raised his head again and gave me a one-sided smile. 'I wouldn't like to live through that again!'

'Nor would I!' said Kate violently.

Mike looked over at her, still gripping my hands.

'But what *happened*?'

'The "bloody great slab" as you put it landed where we'd been lying half a minute before. If it hadn't been for Emily's quick thinking, that would most definitely have been *it*.' Kate spread her hands expressively and then clutched at the rug as it slipped from her shoulders.

'And where were you, Matthew?' Although Mike spoke pleasantly enough, the hint of accusation hung on the air. My hands fluttered protestingly in his, but he stilled them with a tighter grip.

'On my way back from the golf club,' Matthew answered levelly. 'I bumped into Emily on the path—she told me what had happened.'

Mike frowned. 'On the path?'

'I—wanted to see what had loosened it,' I stammered, repeating stupidly, 'it must have been all that rain.'

Mike released my hands at last and stood up. 'Are you both feeling better now?'

Kate nodded and uncurled her legs. 'A really hot bath and all will be well.'

'I could do with a cold one,' Mike said. I saw that his shirt was plastered against him. He must have come up that path as though the Furies were at his heels—and all because he was afraid for me. There had been a look in his eyes that I hadn't seen before. Oh Mike, I thought despairingly, please don't fall in love with me.

The front door again opened and closed, and Sarah appeared at the end of the passage, halting as she saw our incongruous group. 'Mummy, I thought you were going to the beach!'

'Not any more,' said Kate grimly. 'There was a—a landslide—we just missed a nasty accident. You mustn't go to that bay again, Sarah, it's not safe.' She stood up. 'Matthew, if I could make use of your bathroom, Emily can have the other.'

'Of course.'

Mike helped me to my feet. I was still unsteady on them. He slipped an arm round my waist and gave me a squeeze. 'Come on, old crock, I'll take you to the top of the stairs.'

We set off as slowly as a pair of invalids, Matthew following with Kate. The cavalcade wound slowly up the stairs and came to a halt outside my room.

Mike said, 'Since our afternoon on the beach was a write-off, may I come round this evening, long-lost cousin?'

Out of the corner of my eye I caught Matthew's involuntary movement of protest. But Kate was saying, 'Of course, darling, that would be lovely.'

'See you!' Mike said. He bent forward and

kissed my cheek, raised a hand in farewell, and ran back down the stairs.

I went into my room, a lot of half-formed queries jostling in my head. Last night had been, in Mike's opinion, 'one hell of an evening', so why did he want a repeat? And, overriding everything else, whose cigarette lay ground into the grass by the clifftop?

I came out of my room en route for the bathroom. Matthew's door stood open, as did that of his en suite bathroom. As I closed the main bathroom door I heard Kate come out of the guest room, tap lightly on his door, and say with a laugh in her voice, 'This is just like old times!'

I slid the bolt with suppressed violence and turned the taps on full.

CHAPTER ELEVEN

The wind was getting up by the time Mike returned, and I was alone in the sitting-room. There had been no sign of either Matthew or Kate. He came over to the fire.

'How do you feel, sweetheart?' he asked.

'All right, really.'

'The more I think about what happened, the more horrendous it seems. You could both have been killed.'

'We very nearly were.'

'Is Kate OK?'

'I haven't seen her since you left.'

'Did she say any more about the family secret she's supposed to have unearthed?'

I shook my head.

'Matthew would loathe anything detrimental getting into the press. *Noblesse oblige,* and all that. There have been Haigs at Touchstone for a hundred years and they think they own the whole county.'

The door opened and Matthew and Kate came in together. She was still pale, a fact that her make-up could not disguise, and her eyes were feverishly bright.

'Pour me a drink, darling,' she said to Matthew. 'If ever I needed one, it's now!'

Matthew went in silence to the cabinet. 'Sherry for Emily, vodka for Kate, beer for Mike?'

'Correct.' Mike answered for the three of us. I saw that Matthew poured himself a tot of neat whisky. Mike pulled up a chair for Kate, and while they were talking together, Matthew brought me my glass.

'Emily.' He spoke quietly and his voice had an undercurrent of urgency. 'I've been along to examine the cliff. Several of the boulders are loose—the whole face is unsafe. I'm roping off the bay altogether until we can get it blasted properly. I wanted you to know—I had the impression that you thought—that you felt it might not have been an accident.'

My heart jerked, but I met his eyes in silence. He went on, 'It was, though. That's just the way landslides start.'

'Yes,' I said through parched lips.

He looked at me oddly. 'I just wanted to set your mind at rest.'

He paused, then turned away to see to the other drinks. I hoped fervently that he was right. But what of the cigarette stub and the tell-tale crushed grass beside the path?

'Come and join us, Emily,' Kate called from across the room. 'I promise not to monopolise Mike tonight!' She laughed feverishly. 'I must say, this is the most exciting weekend I've ever had at Touchstone!'

'The kind of excitement we could do without,' Matthew returned drily.

'Oh, I don't know; anything's better than that unending monotony! Oh, Matt!' She reached up and caught his hand and I saw his eyes flicker at the obviously once-familiar name. 'I didn't mean that the way it sounded, darling! I'm going to try very hard not to annoy you tonight!'

Matthew's mouth twitched. 'You never "annoy" me, Kate, just as you never bored me. A pity you can't return the compliment.'

'Well, whatever.' She still held his hand, gazing up at him provocatively. 'I promise to be on my best behaviour. How's that?'

He stood looking down at her, then gently disengaged his hand. 'Admirable, I should think,' he said.

I wondered what she was up to, and whether this change of attitude resulted from my telling her Mike thought he wanted her back.

Whatever the reason, I didn't like it. I didn't trust Kate, or the effect she had on Matthew. If he really wanted her, would she come, or did she only want to tantalize him? I suspected the latter, and was disturbed. He had been hurt enough already.

Mike came and joined me on the sofa. 'Cheer up, Emily, it might never happen!'

I looked at him sharply; his remark was altogether too apposite. He nodded towards Matthew and Kate. 'Aren't we pally tonight?' he said in my ear. 'To see them now, you'd never think—' he broke off.

'Think what?'

'Nothing, my pet, nothing at all.'

As the evening wore on, I tried to concentrate on Kate's laughing anecdotes, but gradually my head began to throb and by half-past nine I had one of the worst headaches of my life.

'Honey, what is it? You're as white as a sheet.' Mike had finally noticed my face.

'Probably reaction. I've got a blinding headache. Would you mind if I went to bed?'

'Of course not—we all need an early night tonight.'

Mike came into the hall with me and took my face gently between his hands. 'Goodnight, love. See you tomorrow?'

I smiled and moved away from him. 'Have you no work to do on that farm of yours?'

'Simkins can manage without me. I'll try to slip over during the afternoon.'

I nodded and started up the stairs. He watched me for a moment, then I heard him go back into the sitting-room.

I walked across my bedroom without putting on the light, opened the window, and leaned out into the wild night. The wind seized my hair and whipped it stingingly across my face. I snatched it to one side and held it with my hand, lifting my throbbing forehead to the blessedly cool caress.

Above me, tattered black clouds scuttered across a sky of polished steel and the moon seemed to rock crazily like a silver boat. Down in the garden the trees thrashed, frantic ballerinas flinging their branches from side to side in an anguish of supplication. Above the shrieking and moaning of the wind, the crash of the sea reached me. It would be full tide just about now. I imagined the churning, foam-topped waves sailing into the bay and washing over the murderous boulder that lay there. A spurt of rain spattered on my face like sudden tears. I breathed deeply, revelling in the earthy smell of the garden below me and the tang of seaweed in the salt-laden air.

When I finally closed the window, my hair was tangled and my head still ached, but I felt a little better. I undressed, washed, and lay down on the bed, listening to the sounds of the gale and thinking over the day's happenings. In my mind's eye the cigarette stub glowed luminously in the dark. Matthew had been very insistent that I should agree it was an accident. I shut my mind to that train of thought and saw again the vulnerable look in Mike's eyes as he knelt at my feet. No, I didn't want to think about that, either. Matthew and Kate, Matthew and Kate, ticked the clock beside my bed. There must be something I could bear to think about! Resolutely, I turned on my side and closed my eyes.

I was drifting in the limbo between wakefulness and sleep when directly below me I heard the front door slam. I leapt out of bed and over to the window. Mike was walking quickly to his car, head bent and coat collar turned up against the now heavy rain. The wind must have snatched the door out of his hand.

I watched him climb in and a moment later the headlights flowered in the streaming darkness. The car turned slowly, the great arc of lights sweeping prodigally over trees and drenched flower-beds, setting grotesque shadows leaping on the momentarily lit lawns. As the light swung towards the house, I pressed back lest my white face should be visible at the window. With a roar of exhaust the car leapt forward and turned right towards the main road. The rear lights shone like two evil eyes, then they too were gone.

Too late, I realised my foolishness in jumping out of bed. I was now wide awake. Perhaps a couple of aspirins would make me drowsy, I thought, turning to the dressing-table for my handbag. It was not there. I frowned trying to remember where I'd left it. It must be downstairs, but if I wanted any sleep at all tonight, I should have to go and find it.

I draped my dressing-gown round my shoulders and opened the bedroom door. I'd no idea what time it was, but a gentle snoring sound came from Miss Tamworth's room.

I had just started down the stairs when the sitting-room door opened, and Kate and Matthew came out into the hall. Matthew went to bolt the front door. Through the bars of the banisters I could see Kate quite clearly, standing in the middle of the hall. It was silly to stand here shivering—after all, I wasn't planning to steal the silver. I slipped my arms into my dressing-gown, pulled it tight, and was lowering my bare foot on to the next step when Kate said suddenly, 'Matthew!'

Something in her voice froze my foot in mid-air, and I clutched at the hand rail to support myself. For my life I could not have stopped myself turning my head. Matthew must also have caught the odd note. He stood stock-still. Then, as I was about to creep quietly back to my room after all and wait until they were upstairs, Kate suddenly and quite literally flung herself at him. I caught the spasm that crossed his face before her hands dragged it down to hers. For a moment more he stood immobile and unresponsive. Then his arms went round her and he crushed her against him.

I turned, stumbled silently up the stairs and through the open door of my bedroom. I closed it soundlessly behind me and stood for a very long time with my hand still on the knob. The draught from under the door washed over my feet, chilling my toes and ankles and creeping higher up my legs, while I schooled myself to forget what I'd seen. It was none of my business—none.

Whispered voices sounded on the stairs, foosteps in the corridor, and closing doors. With an effort I at last detached my fingers from the door knob and crept shiveringly back to bed.

But not to sleep. The events of the day continued to revolve endlessly in my head: the crashing boulder and its choking cloud of dust. Kate's veiled threats. The look in Mike's eyes. Matthew and Kate. And back to the rock again: had its falling been pure chance—or was it levered over deliberately on to Kate and me below—levered by someone who had crouched there watching us while he smoked a cigarette?

* * *

Feeling decidedly underslept, I went down to the library the next morning to find Matthew, as always, there before me. I murmured something, seated myself with notebook and pencil, and waited for him to begin.

'How's your head?' The abrupt question startled me into raising my eyes.

'Better, thank you.'

'You look appalling.'

'Thanks,' I said with dignity.

'Emily, would you rather knock off for today? You had a pretty gruelling time yesterday.'

But I'd had enough of my imaginings during the night; I didn't want to indulge in them all day as well.

'No, really, I'm fine, thank you. I'd rather—get on.'

'Well, if you're sure, because I'd like to make up the time we lost yesterday.'

He pulled a pile of papers towards him, leafed through them, and started to dictate. His voice droned on and on, without expression. My pencil flew over the paper, but I had to fight to keep my eyes open.

At ten to twelve the door opened without ceremony and Kate appeared. 'Good morning, Emily.'

'Good morning.'

'Darling, will you take me to the Harbour

View for a drink?'

'I'm sorry, Kate, I promised to meet Tom Francis; he wants to show me an old manuscript he's found. I'll take you tomorrow, if you like.'

'I might not be here tomorrow.'

He raised an eyebrow but didn't comment.

'And there's something I want to speak to you about—something important.'

He glanced at his watch. 'it will have to be after lunch, then. I must go; see you later.'

Kate still stood in the doorway. He waited for her to move aside, but when she didn't, he simply brushed past her. A moment later we heard the front door open and close. Kate said something under her breath which I didn't catch, turned on her heel and left the room.

I put a hand to my throbbing head. I'd lied to Matthew; it wasn't any better, and my eyes felt gritty from lack of sleep. There was still an hour to lunch, and the most sensible course seemed to be to go and lie down. I'd set the alarm to wake me in time.

In my room I drew the curtains across the open window, slipped off my shoes and lay down under the eiderdown. Within two minutes I was asleep.

The alarm dragged me up from a great depth and it took all my willpower to force myself out of bed. However, by the time I'd washed my face and brushed my hair, I felt considerably better. I had also reached a decision: I would phone Gil and ask him to come down next weekend. If I could talk things over with him, perhaps they would fall into perspective and the sense of danger would fade.

Kate was still in a bad temper at lunch, and as Sarah was back at school, it was a silent meal. I was relieved when it was over, and went straight back to the library.

I worked steadily for some time, then, needing to check some facts, went over to the filing cabinet by the door and began to flick through the folders.

Footsteps sounded outside and I paused, expecting someone to come in. When no one did, I realized it must be Kate settling in her corner, and returned to my checking.

So engrossed was I that her voice, just the other side of the door, made me jump. 'Matthew! Can you spare me a minute?'

I'd found most of the information I needed. I pushed the drawer of the cabinet shut with a clang, hoping to warn her I was in the library, but the ruse failed. Her voice came at the same moment, and its quality was equally metallic.

'I realize it's seldom convenient for you to speak to me, but this time I must insist.'

I coughed, but again I was not heard. Moving hastily away from the door, I sat down at my desk. Surely they'd hear the typewriter.

But I was too late. Kate's voice reached me clearly: 'I just want to tell you I'm getting married again.'

My fingers remained motionless on the keys. If I started to type now, they would know I'd heard them.

There was a pause. Then Matthew's said gratingly, 'I must say it comes as a surprise. Your intention wasn't evident last night.'

Soundlessly I pushed my chair back and ran over to the window. I could escape that way. But the key was missing. I remembered Sarah playing with it over the weekend. Frantically I went down on hands and knees, feeling under Matthew's desk and the book shelves behind it, without success.

'Oh, that,' she said dismissively.

'Yes, that,' Matthew's voice was dangerous. 'Why did you do it, Kate? To prove your hold over me?'

'Emily said you wanted me back. I thought I'd see if she was right.'

I sank back on my heels, eyes widening in horror. This was worse than the worst.

'*Emily* said—?' Matthew sounded incredulous.

After a brief pause he went on. 'Surely the question was academic, in the circumstances? But no doubt your ego needed appeasing, as always. Well, did I satisfy you? Or would victory only have been complete if I'd accepted your generous invitation? What then? Would you have laughed in my face?'

'I was quite ready to go to bed with you.'

There was a silence. My nails bit into the palms of my hands but I felt nothing.

Then Matthew said, ‘I can’t say I envy your fiancé.’

‘It was just the old chemistry, wasn’t it? We always had that, but nothing else.’

‘No, Kate, nothing else.’ Impossible to describe the tone of his voice. It could have been utter despair. I prayed it was not. I crouched behind his desk with my hands over my ears, longing for them to stop, to move away out of earshot.

But Kate’s voice reached me clearly. ‘Let’s forego the hurt pride bit. The point is, I want to have Sarah.’

I caught my breath.

Matthew gave a harsh laugh. ‘I see. You want Sarah. Just like that.’

‘It will be a proper home for her.’

‘She has a “proper home” here.’

She said impatiently, ‘You know what I mean. I thought you’d be glad to be rid of her. Tammy will come as well, of course.’

‘You thought—’

‘Oh come off it, Matthew, let’s not pretend. She gets in your way. You’ve no real feeling for the child.’

‘My God, Kate,’ he exploded, ‘what do you know of my feelings? What do you know of anything about me? You’ve never troubled to find out. And I’ve had enough of these insinuations that I don’t love Sarah. Of course

I do, and I won't have her bandied about whenever it suits your convenience. You didn't want her at the time of the divorce, did you? Remember what the judge said? "Mrs Haig seems to be singularly lacking in maternal feelings. I think the child would be better with her father." She'd have been in *your* way then. But now that you're going to set up house again, a pretty little girl might be an asset; soften up your image. Well I'm telling you—you're not having her. Sarah belongs here, with me.'

Kate said silkily, 'If you're going to be difficult, Matthew, I have no choice but to revert to something distasteful. I'd prefer not to.'

'Revert to whatever you like,' he flung at her. 'You're not having Sarah.'

'Have you forgotten St Catherine's House?'

'I wondered when you'd get back to that.'

'Aren't you even remotely curious?'

'Frankly, no. And if what you're trying so delicately to suggest is either you get Sarah or you print your story, then, in the time-honoured phrase, publish and be damned!'

'But you don't know what it is, do you?'

There was a long silence. Then Matthew said quietly, 'I've a rough idea.'

'Really? Well, how would it be if the story got out?'

'Most unpleasant, for several people. But I'm not going to plead with you.'

'Or appeal to my better nature?' she mocked.

'Have you one? Look, you know as well as I do that Sarah has nothing to do with this. You're determined to print your sordid little story, and there's nothing I can do to stop you. Short of killing you, that is!'

'And I wouldn't put that past you!'

'Am I allowed to know who you're marrying?'

'Stuart Henderson.'

'The journalist?'

'Yes.'

'And what does he think of having someone else's child foisted on him?'

'If I want her, he's quite happy.'

'I see. Well, I'm not happy, and that's all there is to it.'

'I think not, Matthew. I'll take you to court if necessary.'

'Please don't threaten me, Kate.'

Her voice rose. 'I'm sure they'd agree that this is hardly the place for a child—a house where her father brings a succession of young girls under the euphemistic name of secretaries!'

My finger nails stabbed convulsively into my palm. I closed my eyes.

Matthew's voice when it came was shaking. 'Get out of this house, Kate. *Now*!'

I imagined them facing each other, Kate on her feet by this time. There was a long silence, then the sound of footsteps. God, don't let Matthew come in here! My prayers were answered. I heard him stride down the passage and slam out of the front door.

I stood up, waiting for the hammering of my heart to subside. I could hear Kate in the room above, doubtless flinging her things into her suitcase. I went to the door, opened it and listened. No one was about. Miss Tamworth would have gone to meet Sarah and take her to her music lesson. Mrs Johnson, I knew, was shopping in Chapelcombe.

I had to get out of the house, but I daren't use the front door in case I met Matthew. I went through the empty kitchen and out at the back. A line of washing wafted gently in the breeze that was all that remained of the night's gale.

I crossed the yard and walked slowly round the vegetable garden, my gaze passing unseeingly over the delicate green fronds of carrots, the rich coppery green of kale.

A car engine roared into life. There was a scattered hail of gravel as wheels spun furiously, and I rounded the corner of the house in time to see Kate's little white sports car shoot through the gates and away down the hill.

I was still staring after it when Mike turned in at the gate. He too stood looking after the hurtling car, then he turned, saw me, and walked across the grass to meet me. 'What's got into Kate? She came out of that gate like a bat out of hell. Nearly ran me down.'

'I—think she had a row with Matthew.'

He raised his eyebrows. 'Really? They certainly weren't rowing when I left them last night.'

He looked at me more closely. 'You still don't look too good.'

'I had a rest before lunch. I'm all right.'

He glanced restlessly about him. 'Let's sit on the grass for a while. The sun's dried it now.'

I let him lead me over to the hedge and we sat down in silence. Mike lit a cigarette, his hands trembling a little. Kate's car must have given him a jolt, missing him so narrowly. He drew rapidly on the cigarette and the smoke plumed upwards, polluting the crystal air. I slid down on to my back and lay staring up at the clouds.

After a moment he lay beside me, one arm pillowing my head. 'It's a hell of a world, Emily.'

I turned my head to look at him. 'Why so, particularly?'

'Oh, Kate and Matthew and you and me—all caught up against our will in a mad kind of treadmill.'

'You're waxing very philosophical today!'

'It's my mother's birthday. A time to take stock, perhaps.'

'Oh. I'm sorry.' So he had been on edge

before the incident with the car. I would like to have known Mike's mother; that lovely young girl in the painting, so eager for life, who had grown up into the rather sad-faced lady in Sarah's album.

'I wish I'd known her,' I said aloud.

His eyes darkened. 'Oh Emily, if you only had, how different everything would have been!'

I didn't understand, but the hurt in his eyes forbade any questioning. 'Don't be unhappy, Mike,' I said gently.

He pulled me towards him and his lips moved over my face. I lay with closed eyes, comforted by the caress. I think it was then, in the lull before the storm, that the realization which I had been fighting for some time finally stole over me and I accepted it. I was exhausted, mentally and physically, and unable any longer to deny my love for Matthew and the unhappiness that went with it. After the last twenty-four hours it was very soothing to accept Mike's gentle, undemanding kisses on my cheek, with no questions asked.

Still sleepy, I was half-dozing in the warmth, when, from the open sitting-room window, I heard the telephone ring. We both sat up and I said, 'I don't think anyone's in. I'll have to answer it.'

'You aren't in, either!' Mike remarked, and kissed me on the mouth. I pushed him gently away and in that moment the phone stopped ringing. 'There you are,' he said, 'someone's there, after all.'

A minute later the front door opened and Matthew appeared. He stumbled forward and stopped, leaning heavily on the stonework. I felt a clutch of fear and, scrambling to my feet, I rushed across the grass, conscious of Mike just behind me.

Matthew's face was a mask and he seemed to have difficulty breathing. He turned his head blindly in my direction as I seized his arm.

'Matthew, what is it? Are you ill?'

'It's Kate.' His voice rasped through lips like parchment. 'I think she's dead.'

'Dead?' I repeated stupidly, and heard Mike's swiftly indrawn breath.

'Her car's just gone over the cliff. It's blazing fiercely; they can't get near it.' And as I clung to his arm, numb with shock, he added—only just audibly—'God, I didn't mean to kill her!'

CHAPTER TWELVE

My memory of those next terrible days is mercifully confined to brief flashes, each in itself sharp and unbearable: Matthew returning from the inquest and locking himself in the library; Kate's book on the chair, forgotten in her precipitate departure; Sarah's first, uncomprehending protest—'But she didn't say goodbye.' There was Mrs Johnson sobbing in the kitchen and Tammy going about the house tight-lipped and red-eyed, but above all there was Matthew, alone and unapproachable in his shocked disbelief. I ached to comfort him, but there was nothing I could say.

It transpired that it was Benson from the farm who had seen the accident. He'd recognised Kate's car a split second after it came roaring round a bend, swerved to avoid a cyclist, and bucketed its way over the short grass verge to the cliff edge. He had watched in fascinated horror as it teetered on the brink, front wheels in space, before, in slow-motion, disappearing over the edge. By the time his numbed legs had carried him there, it had burst into flames and a moment later the petrol tank exploded. The heat was too intense to go near—there was nothing he could do.

He had dialled 999 from the call-box across the road, and then rung Touchstone, knowing Mike was there and hoping he would break the news to Matthew. It was his bad luck that Matthew himself answered the phone.

The police, deferential and offering condolences, called at the house. Had Mrs Haig been in a hurry when she left the house? According to witnesses, she had been driving dangerously fast. Matthew replied that he had not seen her go.

Had she been upset in any way, might she subconsciously have been 'taking it out on the car'? There was a long silence. Then Matthew replied in a low voice, 'Not that I know of.'

Over his bent head, Mike's eyes met and held mine.

During the course of the next few days, we learned that the car had been so comprehensively destroyed that the laboratory had been unable to trace any mechanical failure. From the severity of the blaze, they deduced that Kate must have been carrying a spare can of petrol in the boot. The second inquest duly returned a verdict of accidental death.

Stuart Henderson came down for the funeral. He was a tall, thin man, considerably older than Kate. I liked him at once. It must have been an unnerving experience for him; meeting Matthew in any circumstances would have been awkward, without the added tragedy of Kate's death.

It was cool and dim in the little church, and there was a faintly spicy smell composed of polished wood and the musty tang of old prayer books. The rhythmic breaking of the waves reached us beneath the bronchial dirge of the organ. The church was full; the Haigs were well known and respected.

It was a simple and moving service. I held tightly to Sarah's hand and, despite my efforts to stop them, the tears ran down my cheeks. I was weeping as much for Matthew as for Kate, but Mike, on my other side, was a solid, comforting presence.

It would have been quick, I kept assuring myself; she'd hardly have had time to realise what was happening. Much worse for Matthew, left behind with his burden of guilt and self-reproach.

And out of the blue came the thought: at least her threat of scandal died with her.

* * *

Somehow, the time passed. I had not, after all, made my phone call to Gil, though my mother rang when she read of Kate's death.

I assured her I was all right. No point in worrying her with nebulous fears, and in any case these no longer seemed so urgent. My sense of foreboding had been amply justified by Kate's death, and no amount of talking to Gil could have forestalled it. I'd long since rationalised Matthew's first, agonised murmur. He had ordered Kate out of the house, and she'd driven off in a temper; of course he blamed himself for her death.

He still walked on the moors for long, lonely hours, but gradually his shoulders straightened and the look of strain left his mouth. And Sarah, with the wonderful resilience of childhood, began to smile again. September slid into October, and still the weather held.

Work on the book was spasmodic. Sometimes Matthew dictated furiously for hours on end. Then the next day I would find the typed pages torn across, with the word 'Sorry!' scrawled across them. And we would start again.

Once he said, 'I realise I'm not the easiest person to work with at the moment.'

'It doesn't matter,' I said. I would have typed the same page a hundred times if its dictation could have eased him in any way.

Even Mike seemed subdued. I seldom saw him during the day—in fact, almost the only times I had done so were during Kate's ill-fated visit. But on my free evenings we went to the cinema once or twice, and for drives along the coast, and on one occasion he invited me for supper at the farm. In all that time there was no sign of Derek and Sandra, for which I was grateful.

It was on the visit to the farm that he said without preamble, 'Before the accident, you told me Matthew and Kate had a row.'

His words hung on the air with a question in them.

'Yes,' I said unwillingly. I had spent a large portion of the last few weeks trying to forget it.

'What about?' he asked quietly.

I looked away. 'I've no idea.'

'Presumably it was to do with Kate's marrying again?'

I didn't reply and he gave a bark of a laugh. 'You can bet Matthew didn't know about it the night before. It must have come as one hell of a shock.'

To change the subject, I picked up a silver cigarette box which he'd said was a twenty-first birthday present and ran my thumb over the monogram—M.C.S. 'What's the "C" for?'

He did not reply. He was sitting very still, watching me. 'Why won't you talk about the row?'

'It was nothing to do with us. What does the "C" stand for?'

' "Charles". Look, Emily, this might be important. Why did Matthew lie to the police?'

'*Lie*?'

'He said there was no reason for Kate to be in a temper when she drove off. We know that isn't true.'

I replaced the box carefully. 'He probably thought it was none of their business. What difference did it make, anyway? It couldn't alter the fact of her death. It's not as though another motorist was involved, who needed to be exonerated.'

Mike said reflectively, 'Those cliffs certainly had it in for Kate.'

'How do you mean?'

'First the boulder, then that. Two "accidents" in twenty-four hours.'

I didn't like the emphasis he placed on the word. It reminded me, for the first time since

Kate's death, that I'd suspected the boulder incident hadn't been accidental. Suppose her death wasn't, either?

'What are you trying to say, Mike?' I could hear my voice shaking.

'Nothing, my love, not a thing. But the way you leap to my cousin's defence makes me wonder if he has need of such loyalty.'

For a moment we stared at each other. Then Mike got to his feet with a laugh. 'OK, OK, we'll drop it. Are you ready for something to eat?' And he rang for Mrs Trehearn. But he had resurrected for me two sentences, both spoken by Matthew. One was 'There's nothing I can do to stop you—short of killing you!' And the other, an anguished whisper: 'I didn't mean to kill her.'

Aware of Mike's assessing eyes, I sat down and tried to eat my meal.

* * *

It was a few days after that conversation that I met Jane. I had gone into Chapelcombe to do some shopping, and with half an hour in hand before the bus home, I went to the Tudor Café. The afternoon was cool, with a mist low over the sea, and the café was surprisingly full for a Monday. There were no free tables, so I approached one where a girl was already sitting.

'Do you mind if I join you?'

'Not at all.' She looked up with a smile and passed me the menu. 'Summer's finally gone hasn't it?' She nodded out of the window at the grey afternoon.

'It looks like it, but we can't complain this year.'

'That's true. Are you on holiday?'

'No, I work here.'

'Well, I don't envy you. Lovely in the summer, of course, but when the mists come in and the winds get up, it's a different matter.'

'Do you live here?'

'No, I'm just down for a long weekend—I go back tomorrow. But I was here earlier on, in July. Very different it was then—a bit of life about it.'

The waitress brought my tea and scone. I was glad enough of another girl to talk to, even briefly. It was something I had missed during my stay in Cornwall. My companion passed me the sugar. 'Where do you work, then? I shouldn't have thought there was much scope down here. At the Bank, are you?'

'No, I'm with Matthew Haig, the writer. He lives here.'

She looked up in surprise. 'I thought his secretary was a tall, blonde girl?'

I felt myself go hot. 'She—left. Did you know her?'

'Not well. I used to see her at the Baths in Mevacombe.'

My heart stumbled before I realised why,

then it started a slow, laborious pumping. I heard myself say, 'I think you must be mistaken; Linda couldn't swim.'

The girl laughed. 'That's what they all thought, wasn't it? Her boyfriend used to tease her, so she wanted to surprise him. She certainly surprised her instructor; he found she'd a natural gift for it. She'd reached the life-saving course when I met her.'

I could feel a pulse beating in my throat. She leant across the table and put a hand on my arm. 'What's the matter? You look as if you've seen a ghost!'

I moistened my lips. 'Are you quite sure we're speaking of the same person?'

'I should think so. Tall, pretty girl—lovely figure. She told me she worked for an author in Chapelcombe. Linda something, like you he said. Look, you're not going to pass out, are you?'

I shook my head. 'Who was her instructor—at the Baths?'

'Curly-haired chap, name of Bill. Rather fancied her, I thought.'

'I must see him.'

'Oh, he's gone. He was about to emigrate to Australia and just filling in time before his ship sailed. But why do you want to see him?'

I owed it to her to tell her. 'Linda Harvey was drowned in the bay.'

'*Drowned*?' She withdrew her hand sharply from my arm. 'But—that's impossible.'

'It happened.'

'Well, all I can say is, it must have been a very heavy sea to have drowned Linda. I tell you she could swim like a fish!'

'It was a calm day.'

Her eyes widened, and in them now was a reflection of my own unease. 'I don't understand how that could have happened,' she said flatly.

'Cramp?' There was desperation in the suggestion.

'It's possible, I suppose.' I could see she wasn't convinced. Somehow, neither was I.

I tried to marshal my whirling thoughts. 'Could you—would you mind telling me your name?'

She looked surprised. 'Jane Birch. Why?'

'I'm Emily Barton. Look, would you be prepared to repeat all this—to someone in authority, if need be?'

'The police, you mean? Oh, now look here, I'm not getting mixed up in anything like that! Not on your life! Anyway, I'm going home tomorrow.'

'But it might be important.'

'You mean it might not have been an accident?'

I hadn't yet formulated it into words, even to myself, and the direct question made me flinch. 'Possibly.'

'Well, I'm taking no chances, thank you very much. If I go blabbing to the police, I might get my own head bashed in!'

I said sharply, 'I didn't mean—'

'Look, dear, I don't care what you meant.' She was fumbling in her purse for some money. 'I'm sorry I ever mentioned it. Now forget it, will you? Don't try to drag me in, I'll deny I ever met her.' She stood up. 'And if you take my advice, you'll do nothing about it either. In this world, it's Number One that you have to look out for.'

She went hurriedly over to the cash desk. At the door, she glanced back over her shoulder, and seemed relieved that I had not moved. Then she was gone. I sat alone, staring at her empty chair. Linda could swim. She couldn't have drowned in a calm sea—unless somebody held her head under water.

*   *   *

Mike said, 'Look, honey, something's the matter, I can see that. Tell Uncle Mike what it is. Are you still upset about Kate?'

I shook my head.

'What, then?'

'Linda.'

'*Linda*? But I thought we got that sorted out ages ago.'

I had to tell someone. I couldn't take the sole responsibility of possibly 'withholding evidence'. Quickly, with my hands knotted in my lap, I told him about the girl in the café.

When I'd finished speaking we sat in silence for a long time. Then Mike said, very softly, 'My God!'

I twisted round to face him. 'It must have been cramp.'

'Must it?'

'Oh for God's sake, Mike, what else? Who could have wanted to harm Linda?'

'Or Kate?' asked Mike gently. 'Or you, for that matter?'

My skin prickled and I moved sharply.

'Emily, what are you going to do?'

'I was hoping you would tell me.'

'Quite honestly, I don't see what you *can* do. It's a pretty thin story, without any confirmation. The instructor has conveniently gone to Australia, and Jane isn't going to back you up. All it would do is create more unpleasantness for Matthew, and I think he's had as much as he can take.'

'I know.'

'Of course, if you feel you should—'

'No, no!' I shook my head several times. 'I just wanted to talk it over with someone, that's all.'

'Poor love, what a time you're having down here! Emily—promise me something.'

'Yes?'

'Take care of yourself. I mean that. Take very good care of yourself. It might be better not to mention to Matthew that you met this girl.'

I didn't think it necessary to tell him that I had no intention of doing so.

CHAPTER THIRTEEN

It was Saturday again, a mild, golden October day. Sarah was spending the day with a school friend. People had rallied round very kindly after her mother's death, and her time was fully occupied. I was glad for her sake, though I missed her company, and my free afternoons were sometimes unbearably long.

Matthew had already left for the pub and I was sorting through some papers when there was a tapping on the French window and Mike stood smiling at me. I went across and let him in.

'How's my girl today?'

'Not too bad.'

'Ready for some exercise?'

'Exercise?' I repeated cautiously.

'I thought we might go for a walk this afternoon, along the coast, and if you're free this evening, we needn't hurry back.

'That would be lovely.'

'Good. I've jobs to finish off, so meet me at the gate at half-past three. I'll ask Mrs Trehearn to pack up a picnic.'

'I'll look forward to it.' I went back to my desk and continued sorting out the top copies from the carbons, knocking them gently on the flat surface to shape them into neat piles. Then I carried them over to Matthew's desk.

'The morning's work?' Mike enquired, watching me.

'Yes; he likes to read them through before we start on the next lot.'

I opened the lower right-hand desk drawer where the completed pages lay, and dropped the new ones neatly on top.

'*Fait accompli*!' I said.

He put his hands on my shoulders and studied my face. I looked steadily back at him. His eyes were more blue than grey today, reflecting his sports shirt. What had Kate said? 'He's too good-looking by half. It ensures that he always gets his own way.'

'A penny for your thoughts!'

I moved under his hands and he dropped them. 'I was just thinking,' I replied with a touch of asperity, 'that you're the answer to a maiden's prayer!' And wondering, my mind added, why all your gentle, practised love-making doesn't move me half as much as Matthew's single passionate and irritable kiss. The tail end of the thought caught me by surprise—I was schooling myself not to think about Matthew—and the colour rushed to my face as though I'd spoken aloud.

Mike laughed, naturally attributing the blush to my comment. 'Any maiden in particular?' he asked.

'All of them, I've no doubt.'

'Well, this is the one I have my sights on!' He flicked thumb and finger gently against my cheek and the gong sounded for lunch. 'See you later, sweetheart.'

We set off as planned at three-thirty, down the path towards the sea and across the road on to the springy turf. Directly opposite we could see the 'Danger' notice barring the usual way down to the bay. We turned left and walked more slowly, the salt-encrusted wind in our faces, our hands linked. My mind was still on the morning's work. The book was coming along well now and today, at last, Matthew had seemed to be more in the swing of it than at any time since Kate's arrival at Touchstone.

'Mike,' I said idly, 'what would make you murder someone?'

As I spoke he stumbled at my side and swore, bending down to rub his ankle.

'Have you sprained it?' I asked anxiously.

'I don't think so. Some goddamned rabbit hole.' His face had whitened.

'Sit down for a while and rest it,' I urged. 'We're not in any hurry.' Cautiously he lowered himself to the grass and I began to rub his ankle with gentle fingers.

'What were you saying before I tripped?'

I smiled apologetically. 'I asked what would make you commit murder.'

'Does that pass nowadays for small talk?'

'Suppose there's a wealthy old man living

alone. You decide to murder him. You go along to his flat and hit him over the head with an ornament. Now, the million dollar question is, *why*?' He reached down suddenly, pushing his hand off his ankle, and looking up in surprise, I saw his face was livid. 'Oh, I'm sorry!' I exclaimed. 'Am I making it worse? Wait here while I run back and phone for a taxi to take you home.'

'I'm all right. You pressed on a tender spot, that's all.'

'But it might be badly sprained. We'll have to abandon the walk.'

'Nonsense, it will ease in a minute or two. It'll only stiffen if I don't use it.' He gave me a crooked smile. 'You were asking why I murdered someone.'

'Oh yes. Was it love, fear, jealousy—but hardly, an old man!—greed, or revenge?'

'You said he was wealthy; surely it would be for gain?'

'You'd think so,' I agreed, frowning, 'but he wasn't robbed.'

'So this isn't a hypothetical case?'

'Oh no, it really happened.'

'And you're playing detective? Well, the only other thing I can think of is that one was blackmailing the other.'

'That's a possibility, I suppose.'

He looked at me with a quizzical smile. 'Are you going to explain this extraordinary conversation?'

'Oh I'm sorry—didn't I say? It's Matthew's novel.'

'Matthew's—novel!' He started to laugh, and I looked at him in surprise. 'Well,' he said, 'that's a relief! I was beginning to think you had me on a murder rap!'

I smiled. 'No wonder you were looking worried!'

'Just a minute, though; you said this really happened?'

'The old man was actually killed, yes, but that's only the starting point. Matthew's invented a cast of characters and given them all different motives, to try to work out who might have done it.'

'But who did in real life?'

'We don't know; the murderer hasn't been found.'

'Well, without being obtuse, how will Matthew know when he hits on the right motive?'

I considered for a moment. 'I don't suppose he will.'

'Then it strikes me as rather a pointless exercise.'

'But it's a *novel,* Mike; he's not interested in *who* did it so much as *why.* He's not a policeman, after all,' I added, remembering Matthew's comment to Mrs Statton.

Mike made a move to get up, and I put my hand under his arm to help him. Gingerly he stood, putting all his weight on the uninjured foot. Then he lowered the other, testing it. After a moment he straightened and smiled at me.

'There you are, what did I tell you? As good as new.'

'But you mustn't walk on it—not today.'

'Nonsense. Come on, now, we've wasted enough time.' He took my arm and, not wanting to keep protesting, I fell into step beside him. He was limping slightly, but his colour had come back and I began to accept he'd made the right decision.

A little farther on we came to some steps, and went down them on to the hard, wet sand, ribbed in brown and gold from the receding tide.

On our left the cliffs towered, jagged against the bright sky and haloed by wheeling gulls, while under their skirts lay the twisting caves which bored back into the rock, harbouring cool shaded pools where horny shrimps and angular starfish, stranded by the tide, floated in the shallow water.

Instinctively I moved away from their dank, resounding tunnels to the openness of the beach. The ridges in the sand hurt the soles of my feet and to Mike's amusement I walked cat-like between them. Pebbles and shells rimed the sand where the tide had reached, their jagged uneven line glinting like a broken necklace. I had been collecting pebbles when Matthew had dragged me, protesting, out of the water. Matthew, who had been with Linda the afternoon she drowned: Linda, who could swim.

I shivered and suddenly the deserted beach was no longer a friendly place. Mike glanced at me. 'A cup of hot tea will warm you up. Let's go back on to the soft sand.'

'Not too near the cliff, thank you.'

'It's safe enough here.'

We sat side by side, our backs against a sandhill, eating Mrs Trehearn's ham sandwiches and dropped scones. Mike said, 'This may be the last time; Summer Time ends soon.'

Already the sun was low on the horizon. I looked back the way we had come. The first touch of red was in the sky. The sand had become darker and the cliffs seemed to huddle closer.

'It's the Chapelcombe Show at the end of the month,' Mike said, breaking into my sombre thoughts.

'Oh?' I turned back to him. 'What does that involve?'

'It's mainly agricultural—sheep, pigs and cattle. But there are flower and vegetable entries and cages of rabbits and pigeons and so on. It's later than usual this year because the chairman was taken ill and everything was put back.'

'Are you exhibiting?'

'Certainly; we usually do quite well.'

I held my steaming mug in both hands to warm them. Around us the air thickened perceptibly. He put an arm round me and the warmth of it was comforting to my cold back.

'Do you wish you'd never come to Cornwall, Emily?'

'In some ways.'

'Funny to think if you hadn't applied for the job we'd never have met. I might have been sitting here with my arm round some redhead!'

I smiled with him, but my thoughts had gone back to that day in London when Matthew had first sat scowling at me across a table.

'Since you don't have to rush back, how about walking on to Mevacombe and having a pub meal?'

'We've only just finished tea!'

'That was just a snack, and we won't get there before dark. Are you warm enough?'

'I shall be, walking, but what about your ankle?'

He bent down and prodded it. 'It's bearing up quite well. I must be tougher than I thought.'

We repacked what remained of the picnic in Mike's haversack and started to walk again. The sky had deepened to tangerine and there was a still, breathless beauty about it that was somehow melancholy.

'Have you ever been in love, Emily?' Mike asked me. 'Really in love, I mean?'

'I—think so. Once.'

'I've never let myself. I've seen too much unhappiness, and it's been my motto to love lightly and not too well. Until now,' he added quietly. 'I rather think I've fallen for you, Emily. Much harder than I meant to. Do you think you could ever love me?'

The sunset blurred and sparkled like a prism, and I blinked rapidly. 'Oh Mike, I wish I could!'

He stopped and pulled me to him. 'There's no hurry, darling,' he murmured. 'Just let it come.'

'That—other time,' I whispered. 'It's still there.'

'I can wait.'

If only I could relax and be happy with Mike, instead of always looking over my shoulder for Matthew's dark, restless shadow!

He took my hand and we went on again. A golden wash now suffused our world. High above us a lonely gull dipped and called, swerving down suddenly to the gilt waves and itself becoming stained with the sun's last splendour, a golden bird on a motionless golden sea. The long, twisting pools left by the tide mirrored the sky like golden snakes on the dark sand. It could have been the birth of time. Mike was holding my hand very tightly. There was a waiting hush in the air. Then swiftly, the glory faded, the gold cooled to pale turquoise and the first stars pricked through. A yellow sickle moon swung in the sky. It was a night made for lovers, I thought, and my heart ached.

It seemed a long way to Mevacombe, but at last we could see the lights of its pier twinkling ahead of us, and the cliffs lowered and evened out into a promenade. The town was larger and more tourist-minded than Chapelcombe. It had fish and chip shops, a dance hall—and swimming baths.

We came up from the dark beach into the lights of the town like shipwrecked mariners, blinking in the brightness. Mike was filled with a buoyant gaiety and we swung our hands and laughed along the streets. My ears were nipping now in the evening air but I was still touched with the magic of the sunset.

We turned into one of the old pubs and moved gratefully to a table by the fire. Horse brasses gleamed on the walls and against the bar leaned tanned, blue-eyed men in thick jerseys.

'I'll try the cider,' said Mike. 'How about you?'

'That sounds delicious.' I held out my hands to the blaze.

Mike came back and put the tankards on the table. Sitting down, he raised his to me.

'To us!' he said. 'Don't change, Emily. Ever.'

Later, we feasted on enormous Cornish pasties, which, despite the picnic tea, I managed to finish.

Since we had not brought the car, we travelled home on the local bus. Mike led me to the top deck and we sat trying to peer past our own reflections to where the sea lay in darkness. The bus stopped opposite the road up to Touchstone. It was now very dark; the slim young moon had retreated behind some clouds and there were no street lights up here. I would have stumbled on the rough path but for the security of Mike's hand at my elbow.

'Tomorrow?' he said at the gate.

'Tomorrow,' I replied. I started to walk up the drive, but he called after me.

'Emily—'

'Yes?' I turned back, my fingers already searching for my key.

'Take care.'

'I will.'

The hall light spilled on to the drive. I let myself in and locked the door behind me. The savoury pasty had made me thirsty, and, deciding to take a glass of milk up with me, I pushed open the kitchen door and halted in surprise. Matthew was standing at the sink, and turned when he heard my footsteps.

'Oh, you're back. Did you enjoy yourself?'

'Very much, thank you. What are you doing in here?'

'Trying to repair the damage I've done to this saucepan. I warmed up some baked beans and the light was too high.'

'Where's Tammy?'

'It's her evening off.'

And Mrs Johnson was at her daughter's. Surely one of them could have left him something. 'Have you had anything to eat?'

He grimaced. 'Some dried-up beans. It's my own fault. I'm not usually so moronic, I just wasn't concentrating.'

'I'll do you some eggs,' I said, opening the fridge.

He shook his head. 'Nonsense, that's the last thing you need after an evening out. Anyway, I'm not really hungry any more.'

Ignoring him, I laid the eggs on the counter. 'Scrambled or fried?'

He hesitated, then grinned, and again I was struck by his youthfulness when his face relaxed, as it so seldom did. 'Well, if you insist, scrambled. You'll join me, won't you?'

'I couldn't—I'm full of Cornish pasty.'

He perched on the edge of the table, watching me break eggs into a basin. 'Where have you been?'

'We walked along the beach to Mevacombe.'

'It was a lovely sunset,' he commented.

'Yes.'

I cooked the eggs, made some toast, and laid it out as appetisingly as I could on the kitchen table.

'At least stay and keep me company. It's not very late.'

I sat down, elbows on the table, and watched him.

'This is delicious—it seems I was hungry, after all.'

'What do you usually do at weekends?'

'Open a tin, I'm ashamed to say. When Linda was here—she used to fill me up with spaghetti. It was a speciality of hers—we had a different sauce every time.'

So he and Linda had sat here eating spaghetti. She'd had a 'soft spot' for Matthew, Mike had said. And Kate had wondered if there was anything between them. Perhaps they were both right.

I stood up and Matthew looked at me in surprise.

'If you'll excuse me I'll make a start on the dishes. I don't want to leave them for Tammy in the morning.'

'I'll help you.' He took the last forkful, stood up and brought his plate to the sink.

'There's no need,' I said tightly, and added before I could stop myself, 'Or did you always help Linda?'

He frowned. 'Have I said something to offend you?'

I shook my head, splashing water into the bowl.

'I didn't mean the spaghetti was any better than the *eggs*.'

When I still didn't speak, he said, 'Emily, you're not still upset about Linda's death?'

'Shouldn't I be?' I snapped. 'First Linda, then Kate. I might be next.'

'What do you mean?' His tone had sharpened.

'Only that this doesn't seem to be a very lucky house.'

'No.' He lifted a glass and began to dry it. After a moment he said, 'You don't really believe that, do you?'

'What?'

'That something might happen to you, too.'

I paused, my hands still in the soapy water. 'I don't know. I don't drive, so at least I won't go over the cliff.'

'And you can swim, so you won't drown.'

I pressed my hands down flat in the bowl until my fingers ached. 'Linda could swim too,' I said unsteadily, 'but it didn't help her.'

At my side Matthew became still. Out of the corner of my eye I could see the tweed of his jacket and his hand still holding the glass.

'What did you say?'

I turned my head towards him. 'I said Linda could swim. She was doing a life-saving course at Mevacombe Baths.'

His face was frozen. 'That's not possible. Everyone knew—'

'It was because you all teased her that she had lessons. They discovered she was a natural. She swam like a fish.' I was quoting Jane.

Matthew moistened his lips. 'Then how—?'

'Exactly. How could she drown on a calm day?' I wrenched my eyes from his shocked face. 'So you see I *could* drown, after all. And a boulder can fall on anyone, can't it?'

His hand gripped my arm. 'I told you—that was an accident.'

'Three accidents,' I said hoarsely, 'and two of them fatal.'

His fingers were like steel on my arm. 'For God's sake—'

The clock on the shelf whirred and stuttered and settled back into its even ticking.

'Who told you about Linda?' he demanded.

'I met a girl in the town—she knew Linda at the Baths.'

'But why—'

'I don't know. She was going to have a baby, wasn't she? Perhaps that was—inconvenient.'

'You mean she drowned herself deliberately?'

I paused. 'Perhaps.' But my hesitation had been too long and the alternative was in my silence.

Matthew said harshly, 'You're mad! You don't know what you're talking about.' Then, sharply, 'Have you mentioned this to anyone else?'

'Only Mike,' I said.

'Oh of course, Mike.' His voice was vicious. 'And what did he say?'

Don't go swimming with Matthew. Be careful. Take care.

Too late, discretion blundered to my aid. 'That it was all nonsense.'

'So I should bloody well think. You'd be well advised not to speak of it again, to anyone.'

He flung the tea-towel on the draining-board and left the room. With tears pouring down my face, I finished washing the dishes.

CHAPTER FOURTEEN

I woke the next morning to relentless rain. It matched my mood exactly. The magic sweetness of yesterday had lasted barely longer than its sunset, Mike's tenderness being overshadowed by Matthew's harsh words. I'd known it would be foolish to speak of Linda to Matthew, but jealousy at the thought of their companionship had made me incautious.

I brushed my hair unnecessarily hard. Damn Matthew and Linda and Mike and everyone! From now on I wouldn't concern myself with any of them, but concentrate on my work and leave this miserable house at the earliest opportunity.

Steeling myself to face Matthew, I went down to the library. He didn't even glance at me, but began dictating in that hard, clipped voice which consigned everyone to hell, and I took down his words in much the same spirit. I finished my notebook and went straight on to another.

'No doubt you're seeing Mike today?'

The words had come with no change of tone, and I started to write them before I realised they were for me.

'Yes, but I'll be back at five as usual.'

'I was about to say you needn't be; I'm going out at lunch-time myself and shan't be back till late.'

'Oh. Thank you.'

He pushed his chair back and stood staring moodily out of the window. Streams of water gushed down the pane and the garden was obscured by a curtain of rain.

'I phoned the Baths this morning. They've no record of Linda being there.'

My heart started its slow pump. 'The instructor who taught her has emigrated.'

'Then nothing can be proved.'

I stared at his hunched shoulders and the fear-prickle crept along the back of my neck.

'No,' I agreed after a moment, 'nothing can be proved.'

Something in my voice swung him round. 'So there's no point in going to the police, is there?'

'That's what Mike said.'

He stared at me oddly. 'What I mean is, we've only the word of an unknown girl that Linda could swim. She might even have been mixing her up with someone else.'

'Yes,' I said.

He said harshly, 'You don't sound convinced.'

'It all happened before I came. What can I know about it?'

'But this girl—did you believe her? Is she likely to come forward?'

'You don't have to worry,' I said heavily. 'She made it quite clear that not only would she not come forward, but she'd deny ever meeting Linda.'

Sickly I saw the tension go out of his face. 'Then she couldn't have been sure herself.'

I didn't correct him. Jane had been sure enough, but she didn't intend to be 'mixed up in anything.'

Matthew lit a cigarette and tossed the smoking match into the waste-paper basket. He drew a lungful of smoke and spiralled it at the ceiling.

'So that's that. Well, I might as well go—I've a long drive ahead of me.'

'The roads will be slippery,' I said involuntarily.

He gave me a twisted smile. 'Don't worry, I shan't go over a cliff. Tell Tammy I won't be in for lunch, will you?'

The door closed behind him. I went to my desk and started to type.

The telephone and the lunch gong sounded together. I lifted the receiver.

'Emily? What weather! Are you free this afternoon?'

'For the rest of the day, actually. Matthew's gone out.'

'Wonderful! I'll think of something to do, and collect you about three. OK?'

'OK,' I said.

* * *

The rain was cold on my skin and I was grateful for the roomy warmth of Mike's car.

'You haven't been to Trevenna, have you? We've never gone inland. It's quite a long way, but there's nothing else to do in the rain. It's a pretty little town, up on the moors. We could have tea and maybe go to the cinema.'

'Sounds fine.' I settled back, and we swung right down the hill to Chapelcombe. It was as lonely and depressing as only a seaside town can be on a wet Sunday out of season. Some of the cheap souvenir shops were boarded up for the winter against the ravages of wind and sea. The children's playground raised its bare structures like the scaffolding of some destroyed city. Swings, climbing frames and slides towered upwards, gleaming in the rain, lone skeletons in their surrounding desert of wet, bare concrete.

'Ozymandias!' I said whimsically.

'Um?'

'It reminds me of a poem: "Round the decay of that colossal wreck, boundless and bare, the lone and level sands stretch far away." '

'You're in a funny mood today. Is anything worrying you?'

'No—no.'

'Come on, I'm listening.'

'I told Matthew about Linda being able to swim.'

His hands tightened on the wheel and the car swerved fractionally. 'Wasn't that rather foolish?'

'Why?' I asked, my voice off-key. I paused to steady it. 'Why was it foolish?' I dreaded confirmation of my own fears.

'I thought we agreed nothing would be gained in raking that up.'

'It just—came into the conversation.'

'You were talking about Linda?' He sounded surprised.

'Matthew said she cooked spaghetti for him on Mrs Johnson's nights off.'

'How cosy. Was he suggesting you do the same?'

'No, I'd already—oh, forget it.'

'But what did he say about the swimming?'

'That there was no proof.'

'An odd choice of words.'

'Yes.' It had struck me too.

'Mike—' I had to ask, but my heart was in my throat and I was so tense even my toes had curled up inside my shoes. 'You don't think Matthew had anything to do with Linda's death, do you?' I prayed for a quick, incredulous denial, but it didn't come. 'Mike?' I prompted, turning to look at him. I could see the tightness of his clenched jaw and the hardness in his eyes.

'God knows,' he said at length.

'But you advised me not to go swimming with him, and you said you weren't sure that he'd left her before the accident.'

'In his own words, there's no proof.'

'But what do you *think*?' I asked desperately. The streaming countryside poured itself past us. Cottages and farms huddled under their cloak of cloud. I was reminded sharply, unwillingly, of my drive to Salchester with Matthew. God, it was ludicrous! He *couldn't* have . . .

'Let's assemble the facts and see how they fit,' Mike said at last, and his voice held an undercurrent of excitement. 'First, Linda was a pretty girl who had quite a yen for Matthew.'

I said sharply, 'I thought she was Derek's girlfriend?'

'So she was, but she was always talking about Matthew. It didn't exactly endear him to Derek. To be fair, I don't think Matthew was particularly interested, but she *was* very pretty, and any man's susceptible to flattery. Spaghetti dinners, no less!' His voice was bitter.

I said drily, 'Go on.'

'Next fact. Matthew wanted Kate back.'

I closed my eyes.

'I never doubted that. He was lost without

her.'

'I thought they were always rowing?' I asked faintly.

'So they were. Matthew needs a bit of stimulation—he's not one to fall for sweetness and light. But you should have seen the way he looked at her.'

I had. I said unsteadily, 'Well?'

'Well, when she first left, they were poles apart. Then, gradually, she began to come down for the odd weekend. To see Sarah, she said. Matthew must have hoped that one day she would stay.'

So that was the general opinion: Mrs Johnson's, Mike's, Matthew's . . .

'Well now,' Mike went on softly, and something in his voice sent a shiver down my spine, 'just suppose that, at this crucial point, Linda tells him she's expecting a baby.'

I moved sharply. 'It was Derek's!'

He lifted one shoulder. 'We *assumed* so, certainly, but, again in the time-honoured phrase, we have no proof. The *fact* is that she was pregnant. Now we come to—theories.'

The car purred along, swishing on the wet road. The rain rattled against the glass and the old windscreen wipers creaked laboriously from side to side. With a conscious effort I eased my fingers off my handbag and flexed them painfully.

'So—theory one. Linda told him she was pregnant. OK, it might not have been his child.

But on the other hand, after one of those cosy spaghetti dinners, perhaps he couldn't rule out the possibility.'

'Don't be disgusting,' I said thickly.

'Darling, grow up. Linda wasn't like you, you know.'

'Priscilla Prune,' I said bitterly.

'Exactly!' Mike laughed without humour. 'Well, on the afternoon in question, Matthew goes down for a swim and she follows him. She'd done it before. Perhaps she calls to him to come and blow up the lilo, which he does. Now, suppose he swims out, pulling her along on the lilo. It's a calm, quiet sea, remember. How could the lilo overturn, unless they were fooling around? Suppose that, still fooling, she falls off. Until that moment the idea probably hadn't even entered his head. Then suddenly, there she is in the water—and of course, he thinks she can't swim.'

Against the background of the wet road I could see it all happening as Mike described, and was aware of the taste of blood as my teeth fastened in my lip.

'It's too easy,' he was saying. 'All he has to do is leave her. At first she probably laughs and splashes, carrying on the pretence that she can't swim, waiting for him to rescue her. Then she sees his face, watching—waiting—for her to drown. She panics and starts to swim frantically. But look at the position he's in; she knows he intended to let her drown. So—'

Mike lifted his hands fractionally from the wheel in a horrible, all too explicit gesture. I sat without moving, almost without breathing, my eyes staring achingly ahead. He had made it sound so plausible. But I wouldn't accept it—I couldn't.

'I don't believe it,' I said flatly.

'So,' he went on, as though I hadn't spoken, 'we come to Kate.'

I swung round as though pulled by a string. 'Mike, what are you saying?'

'Facts first.' His voice was trembling with the nervous undercurrent, his eyes almost glassy on the road ahead. 'For some reason best known to herself, Kate decides, the night before her death, to turn on the sweetness. She purrs over Matthew, flatters him, cajoles him, till he doesn't know whether he's on his head or his heels. What happened after I left I don't know, but I've a pretty good idea the guest-room wasn't used that night.'

There, at least, he was wrong, as I'd learned from my unwilling eavesdropping. But I was powerless to interrupt now, listening in fascinated horror to Mike's diabolical 'theory'.

'So,' he went on, 'old Matthew thinks he's home and dry, and everything in the garden's lovely. And then, *then* they have this colossal row. I still think you know more than you admit about it, but in my opinion, Kate calmly turned round and announced that she was going to marry this Henderson character.'

I couldn't deny that, even to myself.

'Imagine how Matthew must have felt. He'd killed Linda to get Kate, everything had seemed to be going his way. She had been all lovely-dovey—then this! Well, he's got a violent temper, you know. Remember what he said after the phone call? "I didn't mean to kill her".'

So he had heard that, too. 'But it was just shock. You can't seriously be suggesting that Matthew killed Kate as well?'

Only when I'd spoken did I realise that the words implied my semi-acceptance of Linda's murder. I said quickly, to cover it, 'How could he, anyway? He was at the house—we saw him.'

Mike didn't speak. Again, almost fearfully, I turned to look at him.

'Well, wasn't he?' I persisted frantically. Still silence. Now my own brain was following the same twisted, tortuous paths as Mike's.

'You mean,' I whispered, 'he did something to the car before she left?' I remembered the front door slamming behind him, and closed my eyes.

Mike moved suddenly, like someone coming out of a trance.

'Tune in tomorrow for the next thrilling instalment!'

My eyes flew open. His joking tone shocked me inexpressibly, like a sluice of cold water on a sun-warmed body.

'You mean you weren't serious?'

He gave a short laugh. 'My dear Emily, one doesn't go about accusing one's own cousin of murder, now does one? It was purely a mental exercise to pass the journey, which it did admirably, because here we are in Trevenna.'

He drove through the wet, deserted streets to the carpark and I reached for my umbrella. A huge sycamore towered over one corner, and its fallen leaves lay spread on the dark tarmac like large golden stars.

Mike took my arm. 'You look as though you could do with a cuppa. Let's see if we can find one.'

I couldn't rally as swiftly as he had, and my brain was still numbed by his 'imaginings'. Because, imaginings or not, they fitted together horribly well.

Mike bought a local paper from a news stand, and when we were seated in a steamy café, he opened it and turned to the entertainments page. 'What kind of film shall we go for? That new thriller—'

'A comedy,' I said decidedly. 'I'm in need of one.'

'There's a Hollywood musical at the Odeon—how about that? Doors open at five on Sundays. We should be out about eight, then we can have a meal somewhere. Sure you don't want to eat anything now?'

I shook my head. 'The tea's fine.' My cold hands were still clasped round the cup.

'Anything else, dear?' The waitress stood over us with pencil poised.

'No, thanks. Can you suggest anywhere we can get a meal later on?'

'The restaurants are closed on Sundays, but you could try the hotels. The St Austell does nice dinners, so I've heard.'

We thanked her and went out into the cold rain.

CHAPTER FIFTEEN

The music crashed to a climax, the hero took the heroine in his arms, and the cameras swung to the distant hills. It was over, and my brief escape into fantasy had come to an end. Beside me, Mike straightened in his seat.

'And they lived happily ever after!' he mocked.

'It does happen sometimes.'

'So does a blue moon.'

'You're a hard-bitten old cynic!' I said lightly.

'Then marry me, and convert me!'

'If you're not careful I might call your bluff.'

'Perhaps I'm hoping you will.'

I smiled and stood up, moving past him to the aisle. Could he have meant it? How would it be, married to Mike? But no, he was only fantasising, as he had in the car.

It was still raining. We collected the car and drove to the other end of town to the hotel recommended to us. It was pleasant but uninspired, and so was its menu. We lingered over coffee, reluctant to go out again into the dark wet night, and again I was reminded of my dinner with Matthew, and how I'd wished it would go on for ever. Yet this afternoon I'd listened to Mike make him out to be a double murderer. Perhaps Mike was right, and cynicism was the safest option.

I glanced at my watch. 'Heavens, we must go—look at the time! We won't be home much before twelve.'

'Cinderella!' Mike teased, but he signalled to the hovering waiter and paid the bill.

The car again, cutting its way through the darkness. For a long time we drove in silence. I was wide awake and faintly uneasy, not comfortable with my thoughts.

Just short of Chapelcombe, Mike glanced at me and without a word drove off the road on to the headland.

'Where are you going?' I was startled out of my reverie.

He slowed down, braked, and switched off the lights. Above my quickened breathing came the sound of the sea. He put an arm round my shoulders, but I resisted.

'Not now, Mike. Please take me home. It's late and I'm tired.'

'Too tired to kiss me good-night?'

Without waiting for my reply he began to kiss me. I went rigid. For some strange reason I felt that I was suffocating. I struggled, pushing at his chest with both hands, and he drew back, frowning.

'I'm sorry—I just don't want to.'

'I wasn't planning to seduce you,' he said roughly. 'I thought I meant at least something to you.'

I reached up a hand to his face. 'You do, Mike, of course you do. But I—I never said—'

'I see.' He moved his head away from my hand.

'Mike—please understand. You don't seem to realise how much you upset me, with all that talk earlier about Matthew and Linda and Kate. I can't just push it aside and pretend it never happened.'

'I'm sorry; it was thoughtless of me.' He was like a stranger, and I realised miserably how much my withdrawal had hurt him.

'Please don't be cross,' I pleaded.

'I'm not cross, Emily.' He started the car, turned it in a wide sweep and we were off the uneven grass and on the road again. In silence we swooped down into Chapelcombe and up out the other side of it. Mike didn't change gear and the car took the hill like a rampaging bull. We skidded round the corner of the road to Touchstone and rocketed up it. I was still wondering how to soothe his wounded pride when I saw that, late though it was, the house was a blaze of light. And, half out of sight round the corner of the house, stood the huge shape of a fire engine.

I tore open the car door and fled up the path, aware of Mike's footsteps running after me. I turned the front door knob with both hands and almost cannoned into Mrs Johnson in the hall. Her hair was braided round her head and she was wearing a blue dressing-gown. Her face was white with shock.

'Oh Miss Barton—' she quavered.

I said sharply, 'Where's Matthew?' There was no time to remember that I was speaking of the man Mike and I had cast as a double murderer. I felt Mike's hand catch at my arm, but I shook him off and threw myself across the hall. In the passage two strange men stood talking. I thrust them aside and flung open the library door on a scene of devastation. The carpet, soaking wet under my feet, was littered with charred pieces of furniture, singed material and piles of scorched paper, and where the curtains used to hang, blackened shreds hung in an uneven fringe.

The acrid smell caught at my throat and stung my eyes, half-blinding me, but I could just make out a figure by the window.

'Matthew?' I gasped. 'Matthew!'

There was a movement beyond the haze and his voice, raw with smoke, said quickly, 'Yes, I'm here, Emily. I'm all right.'

I stumbled towards him and his arms came

round me.

Mike's voice said from the doorway, 'Loath as I am to interrupt, might I suggest you move out of here and close this door? The smoke's going all over the house.'

With Matthew's arm still round me, we did as he said. I glanced apprehensively at Mike as we passed him in the doorway; his face was like granite.

Matthew lowered me gently into one of Kate's armchairs. I hadn't sat there since she died.

'Well,' Mike said, in that new, brittle voice, 'never a dull moment. What happened this time?'

Matthew stood looking down at me. He was in his shirt sleeves. His forearms and hands were thick with grime and there was a smear down his face.

'Are you all right, Emily? Mike, pour her a shot of brandy, would you? Make it three while you're there.'

Mike glanced from one of us to the other and went without a word. The two firemen had moved into the main body of the hall. Matthew and I stared at each other.

'Are you sure you're not burned or anything?' The agonising fear of a minute ago was still fresh in my mind.

'No, really, I'm fine.'

Silence stretched between us, and I was suddenly, burningly, conscious of the way I'd flung myself into his arms. My eyes dropped away from his as the silence became unbearable. Then, to my relief, it was broken by Mike's returning footsteps.

'Well,' he demanded, handing round the glasses, 'what happened?'

Matthew said flatly, 'I came back earlier than I'd intended. If I hadn't —' He broke off and drained his glass. I knew he was thinking of Sarah, still sleeping upstairs.

'And?' Mike prompted.

'There was a smell of burning as soon as I opened the front door. I dashed down here and smoke was curling under the door. So I phoned the fire brigade, then went back to try to fight it myself. I was able to beat back some of the flames but the curtains were burning fiercely and—the desk seems more or less a write-off.'

I looked up, a note in his voice reaching me while it conveyed nothing to Mike. 'The book?' I asked sharply.

Matthew spread his hands in an eloquent gesture.

'*No*!' I exclaimed violently, as though the word could somehow counteract what had happened. 'Oh, Matthew, no!' All that work, the painstaking research, the brilliant characterisation, gone up in smoke. My heart ached for him.

'But you'll start again, won't you?' I demanded urgently, for without the book, there was no reason for me to stay here.

Mike was saying, 'That is tough luck. I know how much work you've put into it.'

Matthew ran a hand through his hair. 'Yes. Well, as I said, it's lucky the whole house didn't go up. If I hadn't come back earlier than expected, it wouldn't have been discovered in time.'

'Matthew!' I caught at his hand and his fingers closed round mine. I saw Mike's eyes glint, but I was past being responsible for my actions. 'You will start again, won't you? You can't let it all go to waste.'

'And rob posterity of a priceless gem? It wasn't that good!'

'But it was! I'll help you—I can remember whole passages!'

Matthew said wearily, 'Two deaths and a fire in the course of one novel tend to give one the impression it was never meant to be written.'

'That's nonsense!' I declared roundly. 'You'll feel differently in the morning.'

'Such faith!' said Mike lightly, and something in his face made me disengage my hand from Matthew's. He made no effort to retain it.

Mike turned to him. 'Is there anything I can do?'

'No thanks, the excitement's over now. Forensics will be round tomorrow to try to find out how it started.'

'Well, if you're sure, I'll be on my way. Good-night Emily.' He gave me a little mock bow.

'I'll come with you to the door.'

'Don't bother. I know you're tired.' It was, I recognised, a reference to my refusal to kiss him in the car, and I felt a twinge of guilt. For despite the tumult of my feelings for Matthew, I was genuinely fond of Mike, and sorry that I had hurt him.

He had turned and started for the door, but I caught up with him and slipped my hand into his. There was no response.

'Thank you for a lovely day.'

He gave a short laugh. 'I get you thoroughly on edge with my ramblings, then I make unwelcome advances. It pours with rain and we get back to find the house on fire. A lovely day indeed!'

We were standing just outside the front door in the deep stone embrasure, sheltered from the wind and rain. He looked down at me.

'I should have believed you,' he said quietly, 'when you said there was someone else. I thought you were just stalling for time, but I see I was wrong.'

I touched his arm in a kind of apology and he patted my hand.

'Good-night, Emily.' He turned up his collar and hurried to the gate, where, in our headlong rush, we had left the car. Last night we'd stood on the beach in a magic world. Even this evening he had asked me, albeit jokingly, to marry him. And how had I repaid him? By refusing to kiss him and running straight into Matthew's arms. No wonder he was hurt.

I went back into the hall, where Matthew was talking to the firemen. I was about to go upstairs but Mrs Johnson beckoned to me from the kitchen.

'I've made some hot soup for the men, miss. Would you like a cup?'

'Oh I would, Mrs Johnson!' I moved into the kitchen, and saw that a door which I'd thought belonged to a cupboard stood open, revealing Mrs Johnson's bedroom. I could see the bed with its with covers flung hastily back.

She ladled me out some soup and I carried it to the kitchen table. It seemed in another world that Matthew and I had sat there the night before. The soup scalded my throat and brought tears to my eyes.

'Could have been burned in our beds!' Mrs Johnson was exclaiming, bustling about in her blue dressing-gown. 'Sound asleep, I was, till I head the master rushing down the passage.'

She set the bowls on a tray, put a plate of bread beside them and moved to the door. I opened it for her. In a moment she was back and sitting down opposite me with her own bowl.

'Such a fuss as you never did see! Not only

the burning but *water*! Water everywhere! Lord knows how we'll ever get that room straight again. And poor Mr Haig's book, all gone up in smoke!'

'It's terrible,' I said, my teeth rattling against the spoon. There were muddy footsteps all over the usually shining floor, where the men had been tramping in and out. A bucket stood by the sink, a reminder of Matthew's own efforts before the arrival of the Brigade.

'How did it start?' I wondered aloud.

'That's for them to find out.' She jerked her head towards the door. 'They seem to think something was smouldering in the waste-paper basket. I'm always telling Mr Haig to use his ash-tray and not fling them matches among all that paper.'

Only this morning I'd seen him do just that. If only we'd known—if only I'd made sure the match was out. It must have smouldered slowly for hours. Then perhaps an extra strong gust of wind would make an additional draught from the window. And the desk was so near.

'You'd best be off to bed, Miss Emily, 'tis past one o'clock. It's a mercy Miss Tamworth and the liddle lass didn't waken—they being upstairs and away from it all.'

I levered myself to my feet. Every bone in my body ached with exhaustion but my brain was unobligingly alert. 'Thanks for the soup, Mrs Johnson—it was just what I needed.'

I went up the stairs like an old woman,

pulling myself along by the banisters. I would have liked a bath, but was afraid of disturbing someone. I lit the gas-fire and huddled over it to undress.

Two deaths and a fire in the course of one book, Matthew had said. And my friends in London had been concerned that I would find Cornwall dull! I was ready for bed but too restless to climb in, and went instead to the window. At last the rain was easing. Beneath me the front door opened and shut, there was the sound of voices. Then the firemen moved into the path and walked round the corner to the engine. It spluttered into life, reversed into the wide driveway, and moved slowly down the path and out of the gate. The lights from below which were illuminating the garden went out one by one. I heard Matthew's dragging footsteps come up the stairs and go along the landing to his room.

I drew the curtains and tidied away the things that lay on the dressing-table, picking up the completed notebook I'd put there that morning, and dropping it into the drawer on top of the others. Then I stiffened, staring down at the eight or nine notebooks which lay there. I had it—almost the complete book—safe and unharmed! I'd kept the pads as souvenirs of my months as Matthew's secretary.

Without pausing to consider the propriety of it, I rushed out of the room and down the corridor to Matthew. I knocked on the door, trembling with excitement. There was a pause in the movements inside the room. I knocked again. The door opened and Matthew stood looking at me.

'Matthew—I've got the notebooks! I'd forgotten all about them! My shorthand notes! Almost the whole novel!'

I'm not sure that he heard me. He said something—probably my name—and then, though neither of us seemed to move, I was in his arms and he was kissing me with fiercely controlled violence, yet this time not at all as though he would rather have been hitting me. It was all I had longed for, dreamed about, and thought impossible.

I clung to him as though I were drowning—and beneath the urgency of his kisses, Mike's voice whispered in my head: *Then she saw his face, watching, waiting for her to drown!*

He must have sensed my withdrawal, because he raised his head, looking questioning down at me—as he'd looked at Linda?

I had to know! I couldn't go on wondering about him any longer.

'Mike said—' I began involuntarily, and then, aware of the enormity of the question I was about to ask, could go no further.

His eyes changed and his arms dropped away. 'What did Mike say?'

For another long minute our gaze held.

Then mine fell, and I helplessly shook my head.

'Go to bed, Emily,' he said.

I nodded and crept back along the corridor, clutching my dressing-gown round me. As I reached my room I heard his door close.

'You little fool!' I said aloud. 'You stupid little fool!' And I knew then that whatever he'd done, I wanted to be with him for the rest of my life. Which was hardly the impression I'd just given him.

Tomorrow, I thought wearily as I climbed into bed. It'll be all right tomorrow.

CHAPTER SIXTEEN

I awoke to find Mrs Johnson standing over me with a breakfast tray. 'Wake up, miss, 'tis half-past ten!'

I sat up hastily. 'But—'

'Mr Haig gave orders you be left to sleep. There'll be no writing done today.'

'Oh, of course.' Slowly memory returned. 'Is—is he up?'

'Lord love you, yes, miss. Up with the lark this morning, he was—hardly worth going to bed at all, as I did tell him. Said he's trying to sort out how much can be salvaged.'

And how much, I wondered, could be salvaged of last night's intimacy?

'I'll be down to help as soon as I'm dressed.'

'Very good, miss.'

I sat back against the bedhead drinking my coffee, and the memory of Matthew's kisses washed over me with hot sweetness. Damn Mike, and the doubts he had sown in my mind.

When I went downstairs, I found that the library had been closed off while a team of forensic scientists sifted painstakingly through the most damaged articles to find the cause of the fire.

Matthew was in the sitting-room, and the room looked like a rehabilitation centre. He'd spread a layer of newspaper over the carpet, and on this were laid various piles of singed papers. There was an overpowering smell of carbon. My own desk, virtually unscathed, had been carried through, and now stood against the side window. Matthew was leaning over it as I came in, sorting through a sheaf of blackened papers.

He straightened. 'Ah, good morning. I'm glad you had a good sleep.' His eyes met mine steadily. 'I must apologise for last night, Emily. I'm sure you'll appreciate that by that stage I hardly knew what I was doing.'

I drew in my breath sharply.

'Also . . .' a wry little smile touched his mouth—'you looked very fetching in your night attire!'

My face burned, but I was incapable of making any comment.

'So now we can both forget it,' he finished briskly. 'I wonder if you'd give me a hand with these papers? As you know, I kept other documents in the desk as well. I hope the insurance policies at least are reasonably intact.'

I moved stiffly towards him. So much for all those castles in the air. It was, after all, a very plausible explanation: exhausted and dispirited, his home damaged and, as he thought, the work of several months lost, he had suddenly learned that, after all, the book was safe. His reaction was simply the reverse of shooting the bearer of bad news.

Now, he was being eminently fair and letting me know straight away that it had meant nothing. One couldn't, after all, let tinpot little typists—the phrase echoed in my mind, throbbing with an earlier hurt—get the wrong idea.

But the way he'd looked at me . . .

I reached out shaking hands to take the sheaf he was holding. As our fingers touched, I felt his swift recoil. Did he think I'd done it deliberately? I didn't care what he thought. Blindly, mechanically, I started to sort through the wreckage.

It was a job that required great patience and infinite care. Some sheets were transparently thin, and crumbled at a touch like disintegrating butterflies. They reminded me of Linda's letter, red-veined in the kitchen fire.

Hastily dismissing the thought, I began with the most badly damaged. Those papers which were beyond recovery, I dropped in the waste-paper basket. Next, I moved on to the singed sheets, some of which had a corner missing or parts scorched into illegibility. These papers would have been in the left-hand set of drawers, farthest from the source of the fire, and fortunately the insurance policies were among them.

'Here they are,' I said dully. I made no move to hand them to him.

'Oh, well done.' Matthew picked them up and leafed through them. 'Thank goodness for that, at least. By the way, did I dream it, or have you really got all your notebooks?'

'I've got them.'

'That's fantastic!' He waited for a comment but I'd none to offer, and, mistaking my silence, he went on, 'Still, I can't expect you to type it all again. Perhaps we could send—'

'I'll do it,' I said. After all, it was my job, wasn't it?

*   *   *

I hardly saw Matthew during the next few days, and for that I was thankful. It gave me time to collect the tattered shreds of my dignity. Also, I'd plenty to do, for, as I'd told him, virtually the whole book was there waiting to be transcribed again, with only the first two chapters, which Linda had worked on, missing.

But that transcription was for the most part automatic, leaving me at the mercy of my thoughts. They were not pleasant company; on that traumatic evening, after hurting Mike more than I'd realised, I had twice thrown myself into Matthew's arms, making a complete fool of myself, and no amount of wishing could alter either fact.

Matthew at least hadn't been hurt by my behaviour. In fact, after our brief exchange the next morning, he'd had the relieved air of someone who has managed to extricate himself with the least possible unpleasantness from an embarrassing and distasteful situation.

Mike, on the other hand, had been since my arrival a good friend and an attractive, amusing companion. It wasn't his fault that I was stupid and wayward enough to fall for Matthew. I spent hours worrying about how I could make it up to him and at least restore the status quo, but no answer presented itself.

Meanwhile, Matthew was sorting out the insurance and supervising the reinstatement of the library. After the forensic team and the assessors, the decorators moved in, and the insidious smell of paint hung in the air. The fire was found to have started in the waste-paper basket, as I'd suspected. I had myself seen Matthew toss still-burning matches into it; I was pretty sure he never would again.

Gradually, as things began to fall into place,

he spent more time with me and our relationship teetered back to what could pass for normal. In all that time I had not heard from Mike, nor found any excuse for approaching him myself. But the theories he had so convincingly put forward on our drive to Trevenna haunted my thoughts waking and sleeping. I would sit watching Matthew bent over his work, and imagine those strong, capable hands holding Linda's head under water or tampering with Kate's car. It was too bizarre to believe, and yet . . . The little thrill of fear eased my battered heart, even if it didn't change one iota the force of my love for him.

'It's the Chapelcombe Show on Saturday,' he said one day. 'Is Mike taking you?'

'I don't think so.'

He looked at me sharply. 'Have you two had a row?'

'No,' I said, stonily.

'It seems a long time since you were out together.'

I hadn't, in fact, been out of the house at all for the last eight days. The weather had been stormy with gale winds, and I had not bothered to make the effort. However, there were now some things I needed, so that afternoon I caught the two-fifteen bus down to the town.

The breeze was still strong, and beyond the shelter of the headland the white-topped waves reared and foamed, hurtling against the base of the cliffs in a fountain of angry spray. The dull thunder of their self-destruction filled the afternoon.

The wind caught me as I left the bus, billowing the skirt of my coat and whipping my hair blindingly across my face. I stood for a moment, my hands deep in my pockets, breathing in the rich salt air with something like exaltation. Above me, the clouds raced dizzily over the pale sky and swarms of leaves, torn ruthlessly from the trees, eddied and swirled in their graceful descent to the pavement.

I walked slowly down into the town, savouring my freedom after being shut in too long with the smell of burnt paper and new paint. Here, the scents were very different, for the wind found its way into the various shops and ferreted out their odours, filling the street with a host of different fragrances—coffee, cheese, soaps, and newly baked bread.

Keeping my eyes on the pavement, I amused myself by identifying by my nose alone the shop I was passing: a strong, smoky smell of kippers, the scent of polish and new leather, the rich opulence of cigars . . .

It was pure chance that I happened to glance into the tobacconist's at the exact moment that Mike, pocketing his change, was turning from the counter. He halted abruptly. So did I. Then he came out of the shop and joined me on the pavement.

He said tonelessly, 'Hello, Emily.'

He was wearing blue dungarees and high boots, spattered with mud. It was the first time I had seen him in his working clothes.

He gestured down at them apologetically. 'I've just delivered some livestock at the station. I wasn't expecting to meet anyone.'

I was surprised how glad I was to see him. Although the constraint of our last meeting had been overshadowed by my feelings for Matthew, it had contributed to my general unhappiness, and I didn't want to lose a chance of putting it right. Even if I couldn't love him, we could surely still be friends.

'Have you time for a cup of tea?' I asked tentatively.

'I couldn't—not in these clothes. Anyway, I really must get back—we're getting things ready for the Show.'

'Oh yes, the Show.'

He looked at me oddly and seemed to hesitate. 'Did I by any chance offer to take you?'

I thought back to that day on the beach. At that stage, an invitation had not seemed necessary.

'No,' I said steadily, 'you didn't.'

He said suddenly, 'Are you really in love with Matthew?'

The directness of it took my breath away, but I managed to say, reasonably calmly, 'Let's leave Matthew out of it, shall we? That's purely a working relationship.'

'Which doesn't answer my question. Oh well, never mind. I've missed you, Emily.'

'I've missed you too.'

He seemed suddenly to make up his mind, and the sullen look left his mouth. 'Would you like to come to the Show?'

'I'd love to.'

'It's held in a field not far from the farm. They're putting up the marquees now—I hope they won't all blow down before Saturday.'

'There's no point in your trailing over to collect me then; you'll have plenty to do without that. Suppose I call for you instead?'

'That would be a help, if you don't mind.'

'What time?'

'Well, it goes on all day, of course, but since someone has to be at the farm, the men usually go along in the morning, and when they get back I go myself.'

'Shall I come after lunch then? About two?'

'That'd be fine.' He smiled, but his eyes were still reserved. He hadn't quite forgiven me. 'See you, then.'

I nodded. 'Goodbye, Mike.'

He went up the road and crossed to the station, where the great lorry was waiting to be driven home. I watched him for a moment then, remembering my shopping-list, turned into the draper's. A partial truce, anyway. I didn't want him to love me, but I very much hoped he still liked me.

*   *   *

The next morning there was a letter from Gilbert. It was to let me know that he had to go to Scotland on business and would not be able to come down as he'd hoped. He trusted all was well and would contact me as soon as he got back, so we could fix a definite plan. Dear Gil, it was as well he didn't know the state I was in.

As I seated myself at my desk, Matthew looked up from the table he was using pending the delivery of his new desk. 'About the Show,' he said abruptly. 'It would be a shame to miss it. It finishes with everyone doing the Floral Dance down the hill into Chapelcombe.'

'Oh I met Mike yesterday,' I said airily. 'He's taking me after all.'

'That's all right, then.' He pushed some papers out of his way with sudden impatience. 'Come over here, will you, and witness my signature on this thing.'

I went over and leaned on the table, watching him sign his full name. ' "Charles",' I commented. 'Does that run in the family?'

He handed me his pen and switched the paper round to face me. 'Not that I know of. Why?'

'Just that it's one of Mike's names, too.' I signed my own.

'Mike's? No, his isn't Charles—it's

something Scottish, after his father.'

'Oh? I thought he said—' And it was then that my eye fell on the book lying on the table. 'Is that Peter Bullock's latest novel? I've still not managed to get hold of it. May I—' I reached out for it, then recoiled as Matthew snatched it out of my hand.

'Give it to me!'

I stared at him in bewilderment, and after a moment he laid it back on the table. I saw that his hands were shaking.

'Sorry,' he said awkwardly. 'I didn't mean to shout. It's just that—well, I've only just got it back and—oh hell, Emily, don't look at me like that. The point is, it's a book I lent Linda. Her mother found it among her things, and as it has my name on the flyleaf, she posted it back to me. There's a note from her inside. I—didn't want it to upset you again, that's all.'

'"Drown Her Remembrance",' I read aloud. The blood was thrumming in my temples.

'I know,' Matthew said shortly. 'A gruesome coincidence, isn't it?'

He pushed back his chair, went over to the fire and flung on a log which had been piled in the hearth. The new wood hissed and spluttered as the greedy flames licked round it, and a shower of sparks shot up. Suddenly, grotesquely, everything seemed to fall into place: Matthew had read a book about drowning—Linda herself had asked to borrow it. A coincidence, he had said.

'Or perhaps not,' I whispered.

'What?' He turned from watching the fire and his eyes met mine. I saw them flicker, take in my words, grow wary. 'What do you mean"?'

I put a hand on the table to steady myself, and could feel the bevelled edge bite into my palm.

'Emily!' He took two strides towards me and gripped my arm, shaking it roughly. 'What the devil do you mean? You're not—you can't be— '

I said weakly, 'I didn't mean anything—it was just a remark.'

'A damn strange one, in the circumstances.' His eyes bored into mine. Then he said very softly, 'Why the hell should I drown Linda?'

I shook my head, but his fingers tightened pitilessly on my arm.

'Come on, you've said too much to stop there.'

The fluttering was back in my throat, beating birds' wings of panic. A tighter grip.

'Well?'

'She was having a baby.' My voice was scarcely audible, but it reached him. He let me go suddenly and I fell back against the table.

'Ah—h!' It was a long-drawn out breath. 'Et tu, Brute! And when—' his voice was gathering strength after the initial shock—'did you dream up this charming little fantasy?'

'I didn't—not really, I—'

'Then it was Mike? A brain-child of my dear cousin?' His voice was tightly reined, but there was some strong emotion just beneath the surface. I didn't dare imagine what it was. My mind wasn't functioning at all. I simply leant where I had stumbled, and his eyes pinned me down like a butterfly on a display card.

'Well now, even if you've decided the child was mine, there's no reason for me to kill her, is there? Or has some subtlety escaped me?'

'Kate,' I whispered miserably.

'*Kate*? Ah yes. You told her I wanted her back, I believe. Really, Emily, you have a most unfortunate habit of interfering in what doesn't concern you.' The words were a whiplash.

'So Linda presented an obstacle to my reclaiming Kate,' he continued. 'Naturally, the obvious solution was to drown her. God, Emily, it's you and Mike who should be writing the novels!'

I barely heard him. My mind was flitting back and forth searching for a means of escape. *You've said too much* . . . The words echoed like a knell in my head. I was nearer than he was to the door, but he'd only to reach out to catch hold of me. Oh Mike, please come! Now!

'Too bad,' he was going on stingingly, 'that it was all for nothing, and Kate escaped my clutches.' He stopped suddenly and his face blanched. I hadn't spoken but he must have read my expression.

'Or did she?'

The room was quiet except for our breathing—his deep and rasping, mine too shallow to fill my lungs.

'And how,' he asked raggedly, 'did I give myself away over that one?'

'Matthew—don't! Please stop it.'

'Come on, what was the criminal's inevitable mistake?'

How could I remind him of his tortured whisper in the porch? I shook my head blindly but he was inexorable.

'I'm waiting.'

I faltered, 'When we heard—when Benson phoned—you —' I couldn't go on.

'God knows what I said, but no doubt I incriminated myself. I'd no idea I'd a recording angel in the house. Dear God, Emily, you've certainly given me the cloven hoof, haven't you?'

'I'm sorry,' I whispered ridiculously. I was torn in half by two equally strong urges. The first was to fling my arms round him and soothe away that numbed look of horror. And the second, perhaps after all the stronger, since there is no instinct like self-preservation, was to turn and run before he could collect himself.

My chance came. He half-turned from me, putting his hand to his head. In the same instant I gathered my jellied muscles together and leapt for the door. As I wrenched it open I was aware of his white, startled face turning towards me. Then I was across the hall and up the stairs two at a time, and at last in the safety of my room. The bolt slid and the key turned in the lock for double protection.

I thought wildly, I won't starve in twenty-four hours. I have some chocolate in my bag. When I don't arrive at the farm tomorrow, Mike will come. Mike will come! I repeated it like a charm. Why oh why did Gilbert have to choose this weekend to go to Scotland, when I needed him so desperately? For the first time I consciously recalled his words at the station, that he would be much happier if I did not come to Cornwall. What presentiment had reached out to him in his anxiety for me—the shadow of my death?

I shuddered. The telephone clarioned in the hall, setting all my nerves jangling. If it was Mike, dare I go down to take the call? Or would Matthew say I was out? In any event, no one called me. I sat on the edge of the bed and tried to stop trembling, feeling very sick. The lunch gong sounded. I didn't move. After a while, Mrs Johnson came and knocked on my door.

'I'm not feeling well, Mrs Johnson; I'll just stay in my room. No, thank you, I don't want anything. I'll be all right.'

All right! A hysterical laugh rose in my throat but I swallowed it back.

It must have been half an hour later that I heard Matthew come up the stairs. His footsteps stopped outside my room, and there was a tentative tap.

'Emily?'

I stood up, staring at the door. A louder knock.

'Emily? I want to speak to you.'

Soundlessly, my eyes never leaving the door, I backed across the room and stood against the far wall. The door knob rattled impatiently.

'Emily, for God's sake, I've *got* to talk to you!'

No doubt he had! The door creaked as he leant against it with the handle turned. I heard him swear softly. 'Open this door!'

Foolishly I shook my head.

'Emily!' A hard shove against the door. Would he break it down, like they did in films? I pressed back against the wall, my hands behind me. A draught from the open window trailed its cold fingers against my neck, and I felt my skin rise in a shiver.

His voice changed, pleaded. 'Please, Emily, I can't leave you like this!'

Leave? I quivered into alertness.

He said impatiently, 'Oh very well, if you want to hide I haven't time to play with you!'

I heard him go to his room and a moment or so later come back along the corridor. This time there was no hesitation at my door. Down in the hall he called, 'I'm going now, Mrs

Johnson.'

The front door slammed, the car revved up and moved out of the drive. I had not moved. I stayed pressed back in case he should look up at my window.

At last, as the sound of the car receded, I pushed myself away from the wall, crept over to the door and unlocked it. I opened it and stood listening. Tammy would be in her room. Had she heard Matthew hammering at my door? Clinging to the banisters, poised for instant flight should the front door burst open again, I inched my way down the stairs and went soft-footed into the kitchen.

'Miss Barton! You didn't half give me a turn! Are you feeling better?'

'Where's Mr Haig?'

'He's had to go to London, sudden like.'

'*London*?'

'Yes, there was a phone call. Won't be back till late tomorrow or Sunday.'

Was it a trap, a way to get me off my guard? But I had heard the phone. Then I had a reprieve!

'Would you like a glass of nice hot milk, dearie?'

Relief made me giddy. I looked at the table where lay the remains of the lunch. 'I'd love a piece of your pie, Mrs Johnson. I feel much better now. But first I must make a phone call.'

Mike's phone rang for a long time. At last a woman answered—Mrs Trehearn.

'No, Miss, I'm sorry Mr Stacey's out. Don't know when he'll be back, I'm sure. He's down at the Show ground.'

I replaced the receiver. Well, if it was true that Matthew had gone to London, tomorrow would be soon enough to see Mike. I went back to the kitchen and Mrs Johnson's pie.

CHAPTER SEVENTEEN

I spent yet another of the restless nights that had plagued me since I came to Cornwall, sleeping with an ear cocked for Matthew's unexpected return. Every creak of a floorboard, every hoot of an owl brought me upright, washed in cold fear. Then, as the sound identified itself, I would lie down again and try to relax. Gradually the window shape became less dense, paled into grey. I lay staring at it unblinkingly, my body taut and rigid. *I didn't mean to kill her—drowning her was the obvious solution—you've said too much* . . . In my mind the words formed the jagged shapes of a jigsaw and how sickeningly they fell into shape. Then, swinging from acceptance to rebuttal, I rejected the whole concept. He *couldn't* have done it—not Matthew!

I jumped as Mrs Johnson knocked on the door. She tried the handle and it rattled ineffectually. Guiltily I remembered I'd not unlocked the door. I slipped out of bed and did so.

'Sorry,' I said, with what I hoped was a convincing smile. I climbed back into bed and took the tray from her. 'I was a bit nervous in the night, so I locked myself in.'

'Very wise, Miss. I always lock my door, being on the ground floor, like. Not that we've ever had any trouble with burglars, but I always say you can't be too careful. Shall I light the fire for you? Quite a nip in the air first thing, these mornings.'

'Thank you.' Sleeplessness had made me shivery. I gratefully sipped the scalding tea.

'Nice day for the Show, if it'll hold,' she commented, jerking her head out of the window. 'It was raining in the night but 'tis passed now, for the present.'

She waddled complacently from the room. I drew a long breath. Well, it was morning at last, and today I should see Mike and all would be well. If only I could have loved him instead of dark, dangerous Matthew!

Before I could help myself the memory of his kisses swamped me and with it a wave of longing which palsied my hand, spilling the tea in the saucer. I set the tray on the table by the bed and got up. It wasn't until I was dressed that I realised that, with Matthew away, the morning stretched emptily ahead. I could do some typing, but I felt too restless.

The solution was provided almost

immediately. There was a tap on the door and Sarah's bright face peered round at me.

'Hello!'

'Hello yourself!'

'Are you going to the Show, Emily?'

'This afternoon I am, with Mike.'

'Oh, can I come too? Please!'

I said regretfully, 'Oh Sarah love, I'm afraid not. We've something very important to talk about.'

'I could wait outside,' she said helpfully.

But we couldn't discuss her father's guilt, knowing she was outside the door.

'Uncle Mike usually takes me,' she added, as I didn't speak.

'I'm sorry, poppet, really I am. Couldn't you go with Tammy?'

'I suppose so,' she said disconsolately, tracing a pattern on the carpet with her toe. Something in the line of her body, the droop of her neck, reminded me, with startling vividness, of Kate, and my heart went out to the child.

'Tell you what,' I said quickly, 'we could go out this morning instead. I'll take you to the Tudor Café for an ice, then you can go to the Show with Tammy this afternoon.'

'All right.' She brightened. 'And perhaps we'll see you and Uncle Mike there, and it would be all right then, wouldn't it?'

'Yes, of course.'

Privately I doubted if we'd get to the Show.

After my conversation with Mike, we would hardly be in the mood for prize pigs and show jumping. It was more than likely that I would be on the evening train, rattling home to London. Come to think of it, I could have utilised the morning packing my belongings. But a promise was a promise, and I knew that when I left Touchstone I would miss Sarah almost as much as Matthew.

We decided to walk down to town and set off hand in hand. I was aware of a feeling of unreality, as though I stood apart watching myself mechanically walking and talking. No doubt it was the result of my sleepless night, added to the tensions of the last few weeks and yesterday's scene with Matthew.

The wind caught us as we came out of the little road on to the main one running down beside the sea. Ahead of us, the twin hotels on opposite headlands crouched like great seabirds landed by stormy tides. Against the cliffs huge breakers rose, flinging up volcanoes of spray.

Sarah skipped at my side, her cheeks stung into colour, her hair blowing out behind her. I remembered my promise to take her on holiday some time. Poor Sarah, it seemed she was doomed to lose everyone who befriended her. Only Tammy remained, with Matthew's uncertain presence in the background. He had told Kate he loved the child but I doubted if she was aware of it.

'Your father's very fond of you,' I said suddenly, and her head turned in surprise.

'Of course!' she said.

'I mean, he might not show it, but—'

She smiled. 'It's all right, Emily, I know he is. It's only that he's always so busy, and I probably remind him of—of Mummy.'

She had said that before, but the repetition took on a new poignancy, now Kate was dead.

'Oh sweetie,' I said contritely, pulling her against me, 'I didn't mean to upset you. I'm supposed to be giving you a treat!'

She smiled tremulously and looked up at me. 'Do you love me, too, Emily?'

I stopped, there on the windblown path, and looked down into her face.

'Yes, Sarah, I do,' I said, with perhaps more emphasis than the question warranted. 'I love you very much and you must always remember that, even if—if I have to go away.'

'Away?' Her face fell. 'But you're not going away, are you?'

I hugged her without answering and we started to walk again. Chapelcombe was unusually deserted for a Saturday morning, and buses that had passed us going up the hill were crowded with people on their way to the Show.

'You going along, then?' asked the woman in the sweet shop, handing Sarah her lollipop.

'Yes, this afternoon.'

'Shouldn't leave it too late; there'll be rain

before dark.' She nodded out of the window to where, out over the sea, purple clouds massed heavily together, lined with gold like great cushions.

Nearer at hand, the mellow sunshine flooded into the shop, pouring its molten gold on the counter and glinting on the tall glass jars of sweets that stood there. 'It's lovely now, anyway,' I said.

'The calm before the storm!' she answered, handing me my change.

Sarah and I were the Tudor's only customers. The waitress, who knew me now, stood chatting beside our table while Sarah ploughed her way through an ice-cream sundae.

'The Show's later than usual,' she said. 'End of September it should be, after the last visitors have gone. Doesn't get dark so quick then. It finishes with the Floral Dance, you know, Jack playing the flute leading us all down the hill and into the Smugglers' Rest for cider all round.' She smiled, rubbing her hands on her apron. 'My Tom reckons that's the best part of the Show!'

Half the shops were closed as we walked back again out of the town. I was more tired than I had thought, and my legs were aching by the time we reached home. Just for a second, as we turned in at the gates, I had the panic thought that Matthew's car would be in the drive. It was not.

* * *

We sat in the big, dark dining-room, Tammy and Sarah and I, and I made a pretence of eating, but the palms of my hands were damp with nervous excitement. The steamed pudding was more than I could face.

'I wonder if you'd excuse me?' I murmured to Tammy. 'I promised Mr Stacey I wouldn't keep him waiting.'

She inclined her head and Sarah sent me a reproachful glance.

'Perhaps we'll see you there.' I hesitated, wondering what possible excuse I could have for kissing Sarah goodbye when she was expecting me back this evening.

'Goodbye,' I said, my voice louder than I'd intended. I was thinking that by the time they returned from the Show, Mike would have driven me back to collect my things, and dropped me off at the station.

The smell of paint still hung in the air. I looked round the hall and it suddenly seemed like home. I shook my head impatiently to dispel the smart of sudden tears, slipped on my mackintosh and closed the front door firmly behind me.

Briskly I turned left out of the gate. The steeply sloping track tugged at the tired muscles behind my knees. At first, I kept my head down, watching for unevenness which might make me stumble and wrench an ankle as Mike had done, but gradually the path levelled and I straightened and looked about me.

Heather and gorse cloaked the moor in royal splendour like a reflection of the purple and gold sky. The ground was springy to my feet after the night's rain, and I walked carefully, avoiding little hollows where the water still lay.

After a while I came to the brow of the hill. Almost directly ahead of me lay the white rectangle of Chapel Farm and its buildings. Over to my left, large splashes of colour indicated the site of the Show and on a gust of wind the sound of a loudspeaker reached me—a man's voice reading out a list of numbers, followed by music. On my right, over the sea, the storm clouds inched forward like an army gathering for attack.

Mike would be waiting. I set off quickly down the hill. There must be an underground stream here, because suddenly water oozed from under my shoes. I moved slightly to one side, then the other, but the ground was wet all round me. I hurried on. The wind-blown music, fast and militant, touched me with a sense of urgency, and the ground sucked at my shoes with soft, obscene ploppings, as though thousands of mouths were gasping beneath me. I shuddered at my fancies.

High above me a curlew called, unbearably

sweetly, and on the side of the hill a sheep bleated suddenly. London would be very different from this. Snatches of music tossed through the air beat against my ears. Hurry, hurry! I broke into an uneven run. The farm lay basking, blindingly white, in the sunshine. I could see Mike's old car at the gate, but there was no other sign of life. The men must still be at the Show.

I opened the five-barred gate and closed it carefully behind me.

'Mike?'

My voice echoed back from the facing wall. I hurried to the farm-house and rang the bell, then, not waiting for an answer, pushed open the door and looked into the dark hall. 'Mike?'

The kitchen door opposite opened and he stood there. 'Hello, Emily.'

I paused, momentarily deflated. In my anxiety to reach him and tell him about Matthew, I'd temporarily forgotten the restraint between us.

'I won't be a moment,' he added. 'Wait in the sittingroom, will you.'

I stood just inside the pretty room, aware of a sense of foreboding. The thick sunshine spilled in a pool on the carpet, but the clouds were almost overhead, giving the light a sinister, pregnant quality.

Impatient at myself, I walked to the fireplace and stood gazing up at the portrait of Laura Stacey. The painted face had Mike's eyes, grey and deep-set, fringed with thick lashes. She looked so life-like I almost expected to see her breathe.

Wondering idly who the artist was, I bent forward to look for a signature. Suddenly my face burned with excitement. Surely—yes, down in the left-hand corner, almost obscured by the folds of her dress, was a tiny thistle. *His little affectation, he called it.* So Mr Menzies, whose murder inspired Matthew's novel, had painted Mike's mother.

Hearing the door open behind me, I exclaimed excitedly, 'Mike, did you realise this is by Cameron Menzies? You know, the artist who was murdered. The thistle was his signature.'

I expected him to hurry over to look, but a strange, ominous silence flowed across the room and pushed almost tangibly against my back. I turned in surprise. Mike was standing very still and there was an expression on his face which jolted my heart into slow, sickening beats.

'Mike,' I faltered, 'what is it?'

'How very knowledgeable you are, Emily,' he said with infinite softness. He started to laugh, almost soundlessly, and the effect was somehow macabre and horrible.

'Mike!' I said sharply.

He stopped laughing and wiped his forehead with the back of his hand. 'That,' he said, 'is the most amazing thing.'

'What is?' I stared at the stranger who stood in Mike's place.

He settled his shoulders and straightened lazily against the door frame. 'Why, that I should have a masterpiece in the house. I could never find a signature, but I suppose, since the man was local, it's not surprising he was the artist.'

'No,' I agreed. Then what had shocked him into this peculiar reaction? The mention of Cameron Menzies? A shutter clicked in my brain. Matthew's voice said, *'Mike's name isn't Charles—it's something Scottish, after—his father.'* Then why had Mike lied to me over such a trivial matter? *and* which Scottish name that began with "C"? *Cameron*? *After his father*? But Cameron Menzies was married for thirty years to Sir Joshua Lindley's daughter.

My skin prickled with fear. There was a connection somewhere but I daren't pursue it. Mike was watching me, an almost abnormal smile twitching his mouth.

'It doesn't pay to be too clever, Emily my sweet.'

I moistened my lips. 'I don't know what you mean.'

'Then why are you looking at me like that?'

'I'm sorry.' I made a tremendous effort at self-control. 'Shall we—are you ready to go to the Show?' I had to get among people again.

He said, so softly I hardly caught the words, 'You're half-way there, aren't you? And once you get that far, you'll soon guess the rest.'

I shook my head violently. 'I don't know what you mean, and I don't want to. Let's go to the Show.'

'You didn't used to mind being alone with me.'

He started to walk towards me and instinctively I shrank back. He laughed. 'Oh yes, Emily, you're on the right lines, so I might as well fill in the gaps.'

'No!' I put my hands over my ears. 'I won't listen!'

'I hear you phoned yesterday; what did you want?'

The question seemed a tangent and I thankfully seized on it. If I could convince him I still suspected Matthew, all might yet be well. The possible link with Cameron Menzies was still too new for me to assimilate. Stick to Linda and Kate. I swallowed. 'You know—you know what you said about Matthew, the day we went to Trevanna? You were right, Mike. He as good as admitted it.'

'I find that hard to believe.' He reached into his pocket and took out a penknife. Then, absent-mindedly, he picked up a wooden ornament from the low table beside him and began to whittle at it. I watched, fascinated, as the pale shavings fell to the carpet.

'Mike, I must get away! I'm frightened!' I spoke no more than the truth. I'd thought myself afraid at Touchstone, where I had Mrs

Johnson and Sarah and my own room to lock myself in. It was as nothing compared with the paralysis that gripped me now, alone in the farmhouse with Mike.

He said thoughtfully, 'So Matthew has been making up more stories, has he? The trouble is, he can't seem to distinguish between fact and fiction.'

'I don't understand.'

'He didn't kill either Linda or Kate, sweetheart, or anyone else as far as I know. Because I did.'

I stared at him incredulously, his head and shoulders silhouetted against the purple umbrella of cloud. His eyes were veiled, watching for my reaction.

I thought: This can't be happening. And then, oh thank God, it wasn't Matthew at all! And then, with crystal clarity: He's going to kill me!

As though he read my mind, Mike smiled, and I felt the breath go out of my body, because it was a terrifying smile, a ghastly caricature of the one I'd seen so often, stripped of its veneer of charm and tenderness; a bleached skeleton of a smile, macabre and unbelievably sinister.

Outside the window the sky was a dusky purple, like the bloom on a bunch of grapes. Somewhere there must have been a chink in the clouds, for still the false sunshine spilled into the room in an almost solid stream.

'Sit down, Emily,' he said. 'I'm going to tell you the whole story.'

I said without hope, 'Couldn't you wait till later? The men will be back soon.'

'They won't disturb us.'

He was mad, of course. He must be. And I was alone with him, with no possibility of rescue. The irony of the fact that Mike and Matthew had now switched roles was beyond me at that moment.

'Well, I'm going to sit down, anyway.' He settled himself on the sofa, one leg carelessly thrown over the other as I'd seen him sit a dozen times. I remained standing, foolishly thinking that if I was on my feet, I might have some fleeting advantage.

'So where shall we start? With your beloved Matthew, I suppose. If you hadn't fallen for him, you know, I shouldn't have to kill you.'

The casual words made no more sense than a swarm of flies buzzing against my eardrums.

'I loved you, Emily, do you know that? Really loved you. But I wasn't the one you wanted, was I?'

'I told you,' I said jerkily, 'there's nothing between Matthew and me.'

'Oh, I know he can be charming,' he said bitterly, as though I'd not spoken. 'I used to see a lot of him, when my mother was alive.' His eyes flickered to the portrait above my head and his voice hardened. 'Then she died, and I realised that he'd despised her all along.'

'Oh, surely—'

'*Despised* her!' he repeated, his voice rising. 'And, worse, pitied me! What *right* had he? Tell me that!'

'But I don't see—'

'Oh, he was careful never to show it, but I know damn well what he thought!' More shavings fell to the carpet, and I watched them in hypnotised silence.

'He must have known since he was twenty,' Mike went on, his knife jabbing at the ornament. 'I'm damn sure his father told him before he died.'

'Told him what?' My voice was almost without sound.

'That my entire life was based on a lie; that my mother'd never married, and I was a bastard.' The brutal words scraped across the room, creating shock waves which vibrated between us.

'Oh yes, Matthew knew all right,' he went on venomously, 'but *I* didn't, because she never told me. I'll never forgive her for that. What's more, he must have been told to keep it from me, because never, in all these years, has he so much as hinted at it. How do you think that makes me feel?'

I could only shake my head.

'But then she died suddenly, without time to destroy anything, which I'm sure she meant to. So, of course, when I went through her things, I found the letters, hidden away at the back of a drawer.'

He dug the penknife viciously into the raw wood.

'Love letters,' he went on, almost unnecessarily, 'from your friend of the thistle.'

'Cameron Menzies.'

'The same.' His voice was calmer now. 'I read them, naturally. Several times, in fact, because I couldn't take it in; and the entire foundation of my life fell apart. I'd not only lost my mother, I'd lost *myself;* I wasn't who I'd thought I was.

'It boiled down, of course, to the old, old story. My grandfather had commissioned Menzies to paint Mother when she was eighteen. He'd have been about forty at the time, already well-known and, naturally, married with a small child. And of course they fell in love. His letters were pretty hot stuff, and reading between the lines, it seemed hers must have been, too.

'Then she discovered she was pregnant, and all hell broke loose. It seems Grandfather went storming over to Mevacombe, where Menzies lived then, and there was an almighty row. Menzies offered to support the child, but Grandfather threw the offer back in his face. Anyway, the long and short of it was that Menzies' wife stood by him, Mother was sent off to an aunt in Scotland, and in due course the story was put about that she'd married and her husband had been killed in a train crash, which was what I'd always been told. All, as I now know, a pack of lies.'

'This was in the letters?' I asked. I had some vague idea that if I could keep him talking, help might arrive.

'Yes; believe it or not, they continued writing to each other, though they never met again.'

'They must have been very much in love. But Mike, why should you think Matthew despised your mother? I know he was very fond of her.'

'But he *knew* about her, didn't he? All the time, he knew.'

It was useless trying to argue with him. Instead, I said positively, 'Well, I'm quite sure he doesn't know Menzies was your father.'

He shrugged, conceding the possibility. 'Anyway, Derek was with me when I found the letters. He'd been very supportive, helping me sort through Mother's things, and of course when I came across them, I didn't know what they were. I started to read them, and it was impossible to hide the fact that something was wrong. I was totally shell-shocked.'

I'd forgotten about Derek, with his hot hands and excitable laugh.

'Mike,' I said gently, 'don't tell me any more, please.'

He looked so much the same as usual, sitting there on the sofa, a frown of concentration as he notched the wood. I tried to forget that it was a valuable ornament he was mutilating, and wishful thinking momentarily convinced me that I couldn't really be in danger. If I could keep him calm, it would be all right.

'You should be proud of your father,' I said rallyingly, 'he was a great painter.'

'But not such a great man.'

'Human, that's all.'

'He got the hell of a shock when he saw me, I can tell you!'

My scalp tingled. This was just what I'd hoped would not happen, the knowledge I'd been fighting to suppress. The odd look was back in his eyes and I realised how foolish my self-deception had been. I was far from safe.

'Derek thought—and I agreed—that he shouldn't be allowed to get off scot-free. We decided I should go and see what I could get out of him.'

'Blackmail?'

He shrugged, not denying it. 'So—I found out where he was living and along I went. There were a lot of people milling about. I went in with a crowd of them and up to the second floor. Menzies let me in when I rang; he was alone.'

His mouth twitched and his fingers, still grasping the little knife, started to tremble. This, I thought irrelevantly, is what Matthew and I had tried so hard to work out—the motive for murder.

Mike looked up suddenly and met my eyes. 'He was a nice old boy—goatee beard and rather long hair. When I said who I was, I thought he'd have a heart attack—his face went all grey.

'He started talking quickly, but his voice was quiet and it was so noisy outside—shouting and laughing—that I could hardly hear him. It was something about always wanting to support me, but Grandfather and later my uncle would take nothing. Then he asked about Mother, and seemed shocked to hear she was dead.'

Mike paused. His words had come unevenly, in staccato bursts, and he was breathing fast. My nails bit into my palms as my body tensed to take what was coming. I didn't want to hear it, but I knew I had to. I, Emily Barton, had solved the riddle of Cameron Menzies' murder, and I wished to God I had not.

I jumped violently as Mike flung the penknife across the room. It clattered against the wall, nicking out a minute tongue of paper.

'It was making me panicky, all that noise, and he went on and on explaining, trying to justify himself. I began to wonder if he was stalling, if perhaps he was expecting someone. So I cut him short, and told him I wanted ten thousand pounds.

'He stared up at me as though he didn't understand. Then he reached towards the phone and at the same moment there was an extra loud crash just outside the door. I lost my nerve, seized the ornament and hit him with it—only to stop him, really. But it was heavier than I thought, and it felled him.'

His voice sank so low that I had to strain to hear him. 'I just couldn't believe it—I was rigid with shock. And when I could bring myself to look down, I saw that what he'd been reaching for was his cheque book, which was lying by the phone. He'd have paid up, Emily. If I'd given him the chance, he'd have paid.'

'Instead,' I whispered, 'he paid with his life.'

There was a long silence. Mike sat staring down at his empty hands. I was scarcely breathing, wondering what he'd do next.

'I hadn't touched anything else. I wiped the vase with my handkerchief and used it to open the door. Fortunately, there was no one in the corridor but the din was still going on across the way. There was a door nearby marked Service stairs, so I went down there and let myself out of the basement.'

As we'd already deduced. I drew a shuddering breath. 'It was an accident, Mike; almost—in a roundabout way—self-defence.'

His mouth twisted. 'I doubt if a jury would agree with you.'

'And, of course,' I was speaking half to myself, 'Derek knew what had happened.'

'Quite so. However—' He stood up restlessly and went over to the window—'there was nothing remotely linking me with it—or so I thought. Till one day Linda Harvey started blabbing about the murder and going to see the old boy's housekeeper.'

He turned and gave me that terrible smile. 'You did that too, didn't you? But you saved yourself just in time—by explaining it was Matthew's book you were talking about. That really shook me, I can tell you.'

I thought back to Mike's ashen face on the cliff, while I rubbed his ankle. I'd been surprised at the time that a sprain apparently severe enough to drain his colour should have mended so swiftly that we could continue our walk. But it had been shock, not pain, that blanched his face.

'*So that* was why—'

'Exactly; Linda's death had nothing to do with any baby. Derek and I used to meet her most days at the Chapel Arms; unlike you, she didn't stay behind typing when Matthew left her at midday, and one lunch-time she started talking about the murder. We were completely dumbfounded. We thought, naturally, that she'd rumbled us, and was going to put the pressure on.'

'So?' My mouth felt dry and swollen.

'So that afternoon we positioned ourselves in the bracken on the clifftop and waited for her to go to the beach. Matthew was with her for a while, and as soon as he left, we went down. She was reading a book about drowning. Weird, that was.'

'Drown her Remembrance.'

'That's it. We thought, of course, that she couldn't swim, and it—well, it all happened more or less as I said in the car that day.'

Yes, it had sounded too convincing not to be true; the fooling on the lilo, the tipping off, the realisation that they were expecting her to drown.

'When we saw that she was swimming,' Mike was saying tightly, 'Derek panicked—damn nearly drowned himself. Pity he didn't, really. I had to hold her head under, and she fought like a wild cat.'

The calm, dispassionate words chilled my bones. Poor, poor Linda; she died not even knowing why. I couldn't bear to think of her.

'And—Kate?'

'Kate,' Mike said in measured tones, 'had been to St Catherine's House and unearthed "a secret". Which could only mean she'd discovered there was no trace of my mother's marriage certificate. However, my birth certificate would have been there, and if it named Menzies as my father, it would link me with the murder. I couldn't chance it.'

'So,' I said with icy calm, 'you tried twice to kill her—the first time with the boulder.'

'Yes.'

'And nearly killed me too.'

He turned quickly from the window. 'I was appalled when I found your things down there.

You'd said you weren't going to the beach, and I couldn't see you from up above—you must have been sitting against the cliff.'

'And when you weren't successful, you came back that evening—to make sure she didn't say any more about what she'd discovered. And also to fix the car,' I added after a moment, 'and for good measure leave a can of petrol in the boot.'

I remembered how he'd come in the gateway as Kate's car rocketed off, and his peculiar manner as he waited to hear of the crash. He'd explained it with the no doubt glib lie that it was his mother's birthday, and Matthew had been blaming himself ever since, because he thought she'd been driving recklessly after their row.

And to crown it all, I had more or less accused him of killing them both. A dry sob rose in my throat and Mike came swiftly to me and took my hand. The grey eyes were limpid and child-like.

'Oh Emily,' he said, 'I wish I didn't have to kill you!'

I started to laugh, tearingly, chokingly, and saw his bewilderment. He put an arm clumsily round my shoulders and I had to steel myself not to shudder. He drew me to the window and we stood staring out at the deserted farm-yard and the beech tree, its red-gold leaves burning like flames in the premature gloom of the afternoon. The first, slow drops of rain, round and shining like marbles, fell with heavy splashes on the glass.

'What shall we do?' Mike asked. He might have been enquiring whether we should go to the Show as planned or, now that the rain had started, drive somewhere for tea. But I knew, by some sixth sense, that as long as I stayed in that room I was safe. Mike would not harm me in his mother's sitting-room, with her gentle eyes watching us.

The rain was falling now in a soft, even patter, and I watched the long globules fill in the dusty edge of the window sill until they merged into smooth, gleaming wetness.

Mike said suddenly, 'I realised that must have been the picture, but I couldn't find a signature, though I searched for it pretty thoroughly. I didn't know about the bloody thistle. Anyway, I couldn't have parted with it—it was a risk I had to take.'

'Yes,' I said.

'Do you blame me, Emily?'

I sighed. 'I suppose that once you'd killed your father, you felt you had to kill Linda. The tragedy is that both murders were unnecessary.'

'I know. Too bad.' The callousness of the words stopped me just in time from almost condoning him.

'And—and Kate; she probably wouldn't have said anything.'

'Oh she would, make no mistake, if only to

annoy Matthew. She was playing cat-and-mouse with him all that weekend.'

Behind us, the clock whirred suddenly and struck three. Then the silence seeped back, broken only by the whispering rain and my own ragged breathing. And I knew that after all I must leave the dubious safety of this room before it became a prison. My survival depended now on the presence of other people, and it was clear what I must do.

I turned to him with what I hoped was a normal smile. 'Can we go to the Show now?' I asked.

He looked at me in surprise. 'What—in this?'

'Yes,' I insisted feverishly, 'please. I want to see your exhibits, and—and do the Floral Dance.'

'In the rain?' he repeated.

'Yes, in the rain!'

He laughed, a high laugh that had in it something of excitement. 'Very well, my sweet,' he said with a terrible gaiety, 'your wish is my command. We shall go to the Show.'

He caught my hand and hurried me across the room, down the tiny passage and out into the rain. I had not time to snatch up my mac from the chair, and Mike didn't bother with a jacket. The wind had risen considerably, but I don't think either of us was conscious, in that moment, of the cold or wet.

The car was standing in the yard. Mike

opened the door and I scrambled inside. It wasn't far to the show ground, but far enough for us to get thoroughly wet, unsuitably dressed as we were. I gripped the seat as we swung round in an arc and bumped over the rough ground.

Around us the day had darkened ominously, draining the gold from the gorse and smudging the heather indistinguishably into the grey-green grass. Mike's face gleamed like wax, and I could see beads of perspiration on his forehead. And still the old car had its comfortable, homely smell of leather and tobacco and the underlying pungency of petrol. It had always seemed a haven to me; was it now to become a hearse?

We bumped down on to the main road, and the crash of the sea reached us over the screaming wind. Mike laughed again, exultantly, and turned left. Perspiration, cold as liquid ice, flooded over me.

'Mike—' My hoarse voice could not be heard, and I tried to raise it. 'Mike—isn't the Show the other way?'

'It is indeed, Emily, it is indeed. You didn't really think we were going there, did you? It was just a ruse to get you out of the house.'

I'd been right, then; I would have been safe at the farm, but only comparatively so, shut in with Mike. And I was still shut in with him, in the bucking car, as we careered over the deserted, rain-soaked moors. I knew despairingly that there was little chance of rescue. My only option was to wait and see what he would do.

CHAPTER EIGHTEEN

We seemed to have been driving in silence for a long time. My mind circled like a rat in a cage searching for escape, for a means of distracting him sufficiently to allow myself some manoeuvre. But, even if the opportunity arose, what could I do? If I managed to get out of the car, I was no match for him on foot and there was nowhere to hide.

I said, as steadily as possible, 'Where are we going, Mike?'

His tongue flicked over his lips. 'I haven't decided.'

A pause. I tried again. 'I wouldn't say anything, you know. We've been close to each other—I wouldn't do anything to hurt you.'

He smiled. If only, I thought uselessly, I hadn't seen that thistle! Could fate really hang by so slender a thread? If Mrs Statton hadn't mentioned it—if I hadn't looked so closely at the portrait—if I'd had the sense not to say anything . . .

He must have guessed what I was thinking. 'Poor Emily,' he said very gently, with that smile still pulling at his mouth. 'What a shame you were just a little too clever—or not quite clever enough!'

'You said you loved me!' I cried.

'So I did, once. Very much. Until I discovered it was Matthew you wanted.'

It was pointless to keep denying that; he didn't believe me.

'And you were very stupid after the fire,' he went on, 'insisting he should begin again on the book. He'd have given up if you hadn't kept on about it. What do you think the fire was for, for God's sake?'

My mind groped stupidly. 'You mean—it was deliberate? But how?'

'I'd seen where the typescript was kept, hadn't I? And when you said on the phone that Matthew would be late back, I got in touch with Derek, and he agreed to do it while we were all out.'

'How did he get into the house?'

'Mother had a key; she used to keep an eye on the place when they were away, and we found it among her things. Anyway, we reasoned that if it all went up in smoke, Matthew'd be too discouraged to go on with it, specially since he'd not even worked out the motive or—' he grimaced—'the murderer.'

His eyes narrowed. 'But not content with flinging yourself into his arms, you had to keep telling him to start again, not to give up. I could willingly have killed you then.'

I realised that he spoke the simple truth.

'I'm sorry,' I said idiotically.

The cliff road was deserted. On our left the rugged rocks rose sheer, their tops swathed in the low clouds, and on our right, beyond the lip of the road, the ground fell away steeply to the creaming, roaring, lashing sea. Already the drizzle was being suffused with the blue of approaching evening. Mike switched on his headlamps and the brilliance leapt ahead of us, funnels of gold on the dark road.

Mevacombe lay behind us, and Tredara, and the little fishing hamlet of Port Perrin. At times, when the road plunged down to sea level, the spray hurled itself over the roof of the car and the roaring darkness deafened us. Then we would climb out of it again, into the buffetting and raging of the upper air.

'Mike! Look out!' I cried suddenly. 'There's someone in the middle of the road!'

He made no attempt to slow down, and the figure jumped clear just in time. Through the streaming window I saw the startled face and open mouth—and the blue peaked cap. A police car was parked at the side of the road. As we flashed past, I wondered if Mike had noticed it. I looked back, and saw it snake out on to the road and start after us.

My hands gripped the seat. Mike glanced in the rearview mirror. 'The element of the chase!' he said, and put his foot down on the accelerator.

The old saloon was no match for the high-powered police car, but Mike's salvation lay in the fact that on the narrow, twisting road, it could not overtake us and flag us down. On the howl of the wind came a new note—the hysterical braying of a siren.

My ribs ached from holding my breath, my eyes were fixed on the light of our headlamps. Oh God, I thought, Oh God! The rock face rushed towards us, swung crazily away as Mike cornered on two wheels. For a moment, as he fought to steady the wheel, we teetered on the brink of the drop and I had a heart-stopping flash of the churning sea, hundreds of feet below.

Mike's face was alight, his eyes shining. He laughed breathlessly. 'How about that, then, Emily? Shall we take a leaf out of Kate's book? We've nothing to lose, have we, either of us?'

I could not reply.

Ahead of us the road forked, the main branch continuing the climb to the left, the right seeming to lead only to a deserted house perched on the cliff.

'Mike!' My hands flew to my mouth. Bearing down the left hand fork came the rushing shape of another police car. They had cut us off.

'Well, well!' he said softly. He wrenched the wheel round and the car spun off the smooth surface on to the stones of the unmade road. In the wing mirror I saw the police cars converge and turn after us. And ahead of us, blocking the track, stood the stone house. We were trapped.

Mike's foot left the accelerator, his other jammed down on the brake. The old car shuddered, slowed. He turned to me, leant forward, and incredibly kissed me on the mouth.

'For auld lang syne!' he said. 'Goodbye, Emily, it was nice knowing you!'

Before I realised his intention he stretched across me, opened my door, and unceremoniously pushed me out. I fell with sickening impact on the uneven track, my left arm bent agonisingly beneath me, lying where I had fallen with my right arm protectively over my head.

There was a shriek of tyres as Mike turned, a scream from the engine as he suddenly revved up, and then, seconds later, only the wind and rain. I lay motionless, the sharp stones digging into my face, holding my breath for the terrible sound which must follow. It was scarcely audible in the noise of the elements—just a slightly louder crash down on the rocks. Then running footsteps and voices. Someone bent over me, someone else said, 'Is she hurt?'

'Not too badly, from the look of her, except for that arm. Mainly shock, I should think. An ambulance is on its way.'

But gentle as they were, the excruiating pain

combined with the strains and stresses of the last few hours, completely engulfed me, and for the first time in my life I fainted.

* * *

I knew that I couldn't move my arm, and also that I was not in my own bed. There was a clean, antiseptic smell in the air. Hospital, I thought bleakly—probably a broken arm. I tried to close my mind to all that had happened, but it broke over me and I made a small, involuntary movement. At once there were sounds across the room. Someone stood by the bed, looking down at me. With an effort, I opened my eyes.

'Hello, Emily,' said Matthew gently.

My eyes filled with tears of weakness. He sat down on the chair beside the bed and took my good hand. 'Everything's all right; it's all over.'

I caught my lip between my teeth. After a moment I said unsteadily, 'Mike?'

His hand tightened. 'He couldn't have known a thing. Really.'

I turned my head away.

After a while I said, 'What time is it?'

'About eight o'clock. 'They gave you an anaesthetic while they set your arm. How does it feel?'

'I can't move it. Matthew, I don't want to stay here.'

'Just for tonight,' he said soothingly. 'I'll

come for you in the morning.'

I closed my eyes. 'Matthew—the things I said—'

'It's all forgotten,' he assured me. I was not used to Matthew's gentleness.

'But I—I more or less—'

'I know, but you had good reason. You were right in your suspicions, you just picked the wrong person.'

Yes, I had picked the wrong person all along the line. Now Mike was dead and Matthew still thought I had loved him. And I was no use as a secretary, either, with only one arm. No doubt I'd be despatched home with as much speed as decency allowed. Following the thought I said abruptly,

'Where's Sarah? I want to see her.'

'She's at home, Emily. In bed. She doesn't know anything about this yet. You'll see her tomorrow.'

My brain felt woolly but there was something I had to tell him that couldn't wait.

'Matthew—'

'Yes?'

'Derek was involved, too.'

'All right, I'll see to it. Don't worry.'

Beyond my vision a door opened and a soft voice said, 'Time's up, Mr Haig.'

Matthew stood up. 'I'll be back tomorrow, Emily. They'll give you something to help you sleep. Goodnight.'

He bent down and kissed my forehead. I

closed my eyes. When I opened them again, he had gone.

* * *

Matthew was as good as his word, and the next morning found us driving sedately back along the twisting road which held such unbearable memories. There were a lot of things I had to know, and sitting beside him, while he couldn't see my face, seemed as good a time as any to deal with them.

'How did the police know where we were?' I began.

'It's a long story, but you remember I had a phone call on Friday? It was from Stuart Henderson, Kate's fiancé. He said it was imperative that he saw me immediately, and could I go up to London straight away. I left after lunch, as you know, and caught the 3.20 train. But we ran into fog and various delays and it was after ten by the time we got there. I phoned Henderson and arranged to meet him in the morning.'

We went over a bump and I winced.

'I'm sorry; are you all right?'

'Yes, thank you.'

We were like strangers, I thought achingly.

'I didn't sleep too well.' He smiled grimly. 'You'd given me quite a bit to think about; I began to ask myself whether Kate's death might not have been an accident after all. Why else should Henderson need to see me so urgently?'

I watched his hands on the wheel and saw them tighten.

'I knew soon enough. He came round to the hotel just after nine, bringing a stack of papers with him. They were Kate's personal things. Understandably, he'd been putting off going through them, but the previous day he'd come across her most recent notes, for this article on Cornish country houses. Lists of dates and names, and then, in capital letters and underlined—LAURA *HAIG—NO MARRIAGE CERTIFICATE!!!* And the word *Stacey* with three question marks.'

So Mike had guessed right. 'Did she find his birth certificate?'

'Mike's? Yes; I don't know who registered the birth, but there was no attempt at concealment. The father's name was given as Cameron Menzies. As you can imagine, I was completely stunned. My father told me years ago Mike was illegitimate—in case a history of the family was ever undertaken—but I'd no idea about Menzies. God, I'd never have embarked on the book if I'd known.'

There was silence between us, broken only by the purr of tyres on the road. Matthew went on in a low voice, 'Henderson said, "I know he's your cousin, but is it conceivable he could have engineered an accident to prevent it coming out?"

'I knew Mike was proud, but I couldn't believe he'd kill Kate for no better reason than to keep his illegitimacy secret. I was about to say so, when Henderson remarked, "The man was murdered, wasn't he?"

'Then, of course, the whole hideous thing fell into place. If Kate's story could point to Mike having already committed a murder, he'd nothing to lose—and a lot to gain—by killing her.'

He paused, glancing at me to gauge my reaction. 'Unfortunately, though, we're no nearer solving Linda's death; the baby—'

'It wasn't the baby,' I interrupted. 'She started to talk about the murder, and they didn't realise she was referring to the book.'

'Oh God!' Matthew said softly, then, with sudden sharpness, 'So *you* might—'

'Yes, I nearly finished up the same way, but my guardian angel made me mention the novel. Which was why we had the fire.'

'Mike was responsible for that, too?'

I nodded.

'Thank God I didn't know all that when I was in London. As it was, I was out of my mind with worry.'

'About me?' I asked shakily. 'The girl who'd just accused you of murder?'

Matthew said grimly, 'For all I knew, you might have made a habit of it, in which case I didn't give much for your chances with Mike. How did you find out, anyway?'

I told him about the thistle, and remembering his saying Mike's name wasn't Charles, although he'd told me it was.

'I knew it was something Scottish, but the connection never struck me. No earthly reason why it should, of course. Well, Henderson and I thrashed it out and arrived at more or less the right conclusion. He insisted that you wouldn't be in danger, because you didn't know Mike was the killer.' A smile twisted his mouth. 'It was strange comfort, to know that you thought I was!'

I hung my head. After a moment he went on, 'As soon as Henderson had gone, I phoned Touchstone, but you'd already left to meet Mike. Needless to say, I'd forgotten all about the Show. I didn't dare phone the farm, because I couldn't say anything with him being there. I caught the 2.30 train, but during the journey I became obsessed by the idea that by the time I got home it might be too late. So I phoned Chapelcombe Police Station from somewhere along the line. It wasn't the easiest thing to get across, I can tell you. Inspector Franklin has known Mike and me since we were boys. I'd never have tried, if it hadn't been—'

He broke off and I sat without moving. We slowed down, turned up into the Touchstone road and nosed gently through the gateway. Matthew stopped the car and sat with his hands on the wheel.

'I phoned again as soon as I got off the train. There was a lot of panic by that time, cars out all over the place trying to head him off. When I heard you were with him—' He broke off and lit a cigarette.

'One of the cars was near the station and they radioed it to pick me up. It was while we were tearing along that we got the news that—it was all over. We headed straight for the hospital. I'd only just arrived when you came round. I've told the police about Derek, by the way; they're dealing with it.'

'And—Mike?' I whispered.

'They sent out helicopters, lifeboats, the lot, but they knew he hadn't a hope. Don't grieve too much for him, Emily. It was better that way.'

He opened the door and came round to help me out.

'Sarah knows only that he's dead,' he warned me as he guided me up the path. 'There's no need for her to know any more.'

As he opened the front door, Sarah herself rushed across the hall and flung herself against me in a storm of tears.

'Careful!' Matthew said sharply.

'It's all right.' Cautiously I knelt down, my good arm going round the shaking little body.

'I thought you were dead too!' she sobbed. 'They wouldn't tell me what happened. Oh Emily, you won't go away like you said, will you?'

I said with difficulty, 'Not just yet, Sarah. Don't cry. Nothing can hurt Uncle Mike any more.'

Matthew detached her gently. 'Come along, sweetheart, Emily's not very strong at the moment. Let's get her to a chair, shall we?'

Sarah allowed herself to be disengaged and Matthew raised me to my feet. At the back of the hall, Tammy appeared.

'I hope you're feeling better, Miss Barton,' she said stiffly. She took Sarah's hand and the child went upstairs with her without protest.

Matthew led me into the sitting-room and I lowered myself gingerly on to the sofa. The room was filled with watery light as the sun struggled to find a way through the clouds. He poured two drinks and I took a gulp of mine. He put his own glass on the mantelpiece and stood with a foot on the fender, staring into the fire.

'Look,' he said abruptly, 'I appreciate that you'll want to leave here as soon as possible, and I quite understand. But—well, you heard Sarah. It's been a great shock to her. I don't want her to lose—both of you—so close together. After all, she's only just getting over Kate's death. It's made everything so insecure for her.'

He glanced at me. 'There's something special between you two, isn't there? You asked for her in hospital, when you were barely conscious.'

'I'm very fond of her.'

'It's obviously mutual. I could hardly ask you to stay on my own account, but—'

I took a deep breath. 'Why not?'

'What?' He turned, frowning at the interruption to what was patently a prepared speech.

'Why couldn't you ask on your own account? Don't you want me to stay?'

He stared at me and somehow I managed to meet his gaze.

At last he said, 'I thought you knew the answer to that.'

'No,' I said, and my voice sounded a little hysterical, 'I don't know the answer to anything—anything at all!'

'Are you trying to tell me you don't know how I feel about you? I had the impression I'd made it only too plain.'

'Because you kissed me twice?' I asked shakily. 'The first time because you were in a vile temper and the second, as you were very careful to explain, because you were so tired you didn't know what you were doing?'

He said 'Emily!' in a strangled voice, and took a step towards me. My self-control was in tatters now. I bent my head and my tears rained on to my plaster with a steady little rattling sound.

He said, 'But darling, I thought Mike—'

I shook my head. 'Only at the very beginning—never, really. After that it was always—'

'Yes?'

He was standing right above me.

'You, damn you!' I sobbed.

Then he was beside me, gathering me gently against him and kissing away my tears and I turned my face urgently to meet his mouth. I was vaguely aware at some point of hearing the lunch gong, and after a few minutes there was a knock on the door. When we did not answer, whoever it was went away again.

At last I moved a little. Matthew raised his head and we looked at each other.

'Oh God, Emily, I love you so much.'

I put my hand up to his face and he caught it and kissed the palm. 'How long have you known?'

'It's hard to say; when I dragged you out of the water that time, I was shaken by the violence of my reactions. It wasn't only because of Linda, it was very much because you, personally, seemed to be in danger. And I certainly was in no doubt of my feelings that day in Salchester. But you touched me on the raw about Sarah, which was why I was unforgivably rude. I meant to apologise the next day—I would have done, but for Kate's arrival. And of course, it seemed to be Mike, from the word go. You were always talking about him going out with him, I told myself it was only to be expected and I tried to accept it. Then, on the night of the fire when you ran to me, I half-wondered—and when you came to my room, all wide-eyed with excitement and in that extremely sexy nightdress—no, darling, I'm only teasing!—I just couldn't help myself. But as soon as I let you go, you made some remark about Mike, and I was convinced I'd made a fool of myself. Hence my rapid retraction the next day.'

'I behaved very stupidly, but that afternoon Mike had terrified me with all his talk of murder and I didn't know what to believe. Also, I was frightened of being hurt.'

'We both were, that's what fouled the works. When Kate told me you said I wanted her back—well, I didn't know what to think.'

'Actually, I said Mike thought so. Matthew—I have to tell you—I was in the library that day. I heard the row with Kate. It all started so suddenly I hadn't time to come out.'

He said heavily, 'Then you know how it was.'

'But you loved her once. And Mike said you took it very badly when she left.'

'I loved what I thought she was. There was a strong physical attraction between us, but little else, and we made each other very unhappy. As to being upset when she left, that was because of Sarah. *She* was heartbroken. Once, soon after Kate left, I heard her crying in bed. But when I tried to comfort her, she started hitting out at me, asking why I'd sent Mummy away. Sarah meant everything to me—you can imagine how I felt.'

I said softly, 'Oh, darling!'

'Well, she was half asleep at the time and she might not have meant it anyway. But after that I was cautious about showing too much affection. No doubt it was stupid, but I didn't want to chance being—rejected—again.'

He smiled at me. 'You'll have to teach me how to get close to her. But even for Sarah, I could never have had Kate back.'

I leaned against him and closed my eyes. I was very tired. 'What will you do about the book?'

'My first thought was to scrap it, but I don't think I shall. It might have helped solve a real murder, but it's fiction, after all; I used only the barest outline of the Menzies case, and as you know, the characters are entirely different. So we'll let it stand as an epitaph, to Kate and Menzies and Linda. Even, in a way, to Mike.'

He kissed my hair. 'And now, my beloved, I think we should at least make some pretence of eating, or Tammy will be mortally offended.'

'Tammy?'

'She's done the necessary today.' And, at my blank look, he added, 'It's Sunday, remember, and Mrs Johnson, in total ignorance of all that's happened, is at her daughter's.' He raised me to my feet and kissed me again. 'So let's go and find Sarah and tell her you won't be going away—ever.'

With our arms still about each other, we moved slowly towards the door.

EPILOGUE

Sarah closed the typescript and looked across at me with tears in her eyes.

'It brings it all back,' she said, 'and fills in quite a few gaps, too.' She paused. 'Do you think Dad really despised Aunt Laura?'

'Of course not. He was a young man, remember, when he heard about it, and he thought it was most romantic. But it did make him see her in a new light—gave her more depth, as he put it. Actually, I think it influenced him more than he realises, and explains why he's so good at portraying women in his books.'

'I suspect,' Sarah said carefully, feeling her way, 'that it was Uncle Mike who despised her, and he couldn't bear it.'

I nodded thoughtfully. 'The trouble was, he didn't have time to get used to the idea. If it had been one of his friends who'd had an illegitimate child, I'm quite sure he'd have been understanding. After all, he didn't condemn Linda. But it was his *mother,* whom he'd always adored and felt so close to.

'He suddenly realised they'd not been as close as he'd thought, since she'd never told him the truth, and coming so soon after her death, it was too much for him. Even so, if Derek hadn't been with him when he found out, he might have come to terms with it eventually. But Derek, being Derek, lost no time in stirring up trouble.'

Sarah laid the typescript down on the table. 'You know, when Sophie said last summer what you were going to do, I was a bit ambivalent about it.'

'So was I, when she suggested it.'

'I'm glad you went ahead, though. After all, it's part of our family history. I can show it to the children when they're older.'

'And talking of the children,' I said, rising and going to the window, 'it's time we rescued your father and David.'

Out on the lawn, Matthew was engaged in throwing a ball to his two-year-old grandson, while Sarah's husband bounced the baby on his knee. She came and joined me, slipping an arm round my waist.

'Of course it's sad remembering everyone who died,' she said, 'but Dad's book also brought you to Touchstone, and that's something to be thankful for, isn't it?'

'It certainly is,' I said.